[redacted]

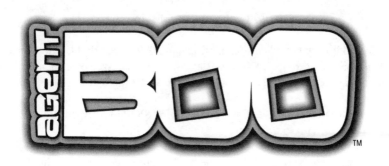

Agent Boo:
The Heart of Iron

manga**chapters**

visit us at www.abdopublishing.com

Reinforced library bound edition published in 2009 by Spotlight, a division of ABDO Publishing Group, 8000 West 78th Street, Edina, Minnesota 55439. This edition reprinted by arrangement with TOKYOPOP Inc. www.tokyopop.com

Design and Layout	Courtney H. Geter
Cover Design	Fawn Lau
Editor	Tim Beedle
Development Editor	Carol Fox
Senior Editor	Jenna Winterberg
Digital Imaging Manager	Chris Buford
Pre-Press Supervisor	Erika Terriquez
Art Director	Anne Marie Horne
Production Manager	Elisabeth Brizzi

Library of Congress Cataloging-in-Publication Data
This title was previously cataloged with the following information:
De Campi, Alex.
  The Heart of Iron / written by Alex de Campi ; illustrated by Edo Fuijkschot.
    p. cm. -- (Agent Boo ; bk. 3)
  Summary: Agents Boo and Asano must rescue Agent Kira, who was captured by Queen Misery and Commissar Noir. In the process, they learn that Queen Misery has problems of her own, and they work toward helping her solve them.
  [1. Science fiction.] I. Fuijkschot, Edo, ill. II. Title. III. Series: De Campi, Alex. Agent Boo ; bk. 3.
PZ7.D35513Lit 2006
[Fic]--dc22   2006013505

All Spotlight books have reinforced library binding and are manufactured in the United States of America.

Contents

CHAPTER 1
Previously . . .

Every kid in Space City wants to be an Agent someday. So, when the Agents come to pick the new trainees from the senior class, it's a big deal.

The animal companions of the fallen Agents pick new recruits to serve. It's no surprise that Quoth, the raven, picked Asano. His brother, Erik, was a great Agent. And Asano was an amazing athlete! It also was no surprise that Seeker, the shy badger, chose outgoing, confident Kira, who was the smartest in her class. But everyone was shocked when Pumpkin, the wily cat, chose Agent Boo—the smallest in the fourth grade class!

The new Agents went straight to Home Base, the Agents' Aerie. There, they started school all over again. This time, though, they learned about the Parallel worlds, technology, and historical battles. They even learned Martial Arts!

After taking the Agent test, the newest recruits were ready for their first mission. In search of the evil Queen Misery, the agents took off to Snow City . . . all but Boo, who was left behind with Pumpkin.

Boo and Pumpkin were enjoying an ice cream snack back at the Aerie when they heard voices!

Boo ran to find out how the mission had gone. But it wasn't the Agents whose voices she'd heard!

Queen Misery and her right-hand man Commissar Noir had tricked the Agents into leaving so they could invade the Aerie!

And they were just as startled to run across Boo as she was to see them!

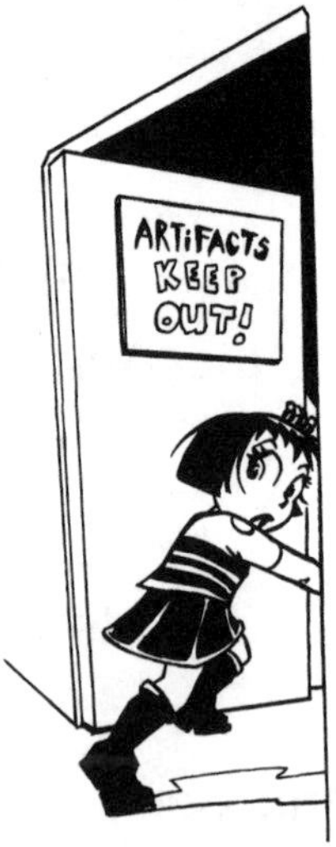
ARTIFACTS
KEEP
OUT!

Being little helped Boo escape—she ducked and ran as fast as she could! Then she hid in the Artifact closet. She hoped the "Keep Out" sign would keep Queen Misery away. But she didn't expect to find a talking mirror—or an Egg Timer of Improbability.

The mirror told her the Egg Timer of Improbability granted wishes. But the wishes it granted were only for unlikely things.

So when Misery discovered her, Boo wished for a very unlikely thing: giant space pirate monkeys in kilts!

And mad monkey chaos was unleashed!

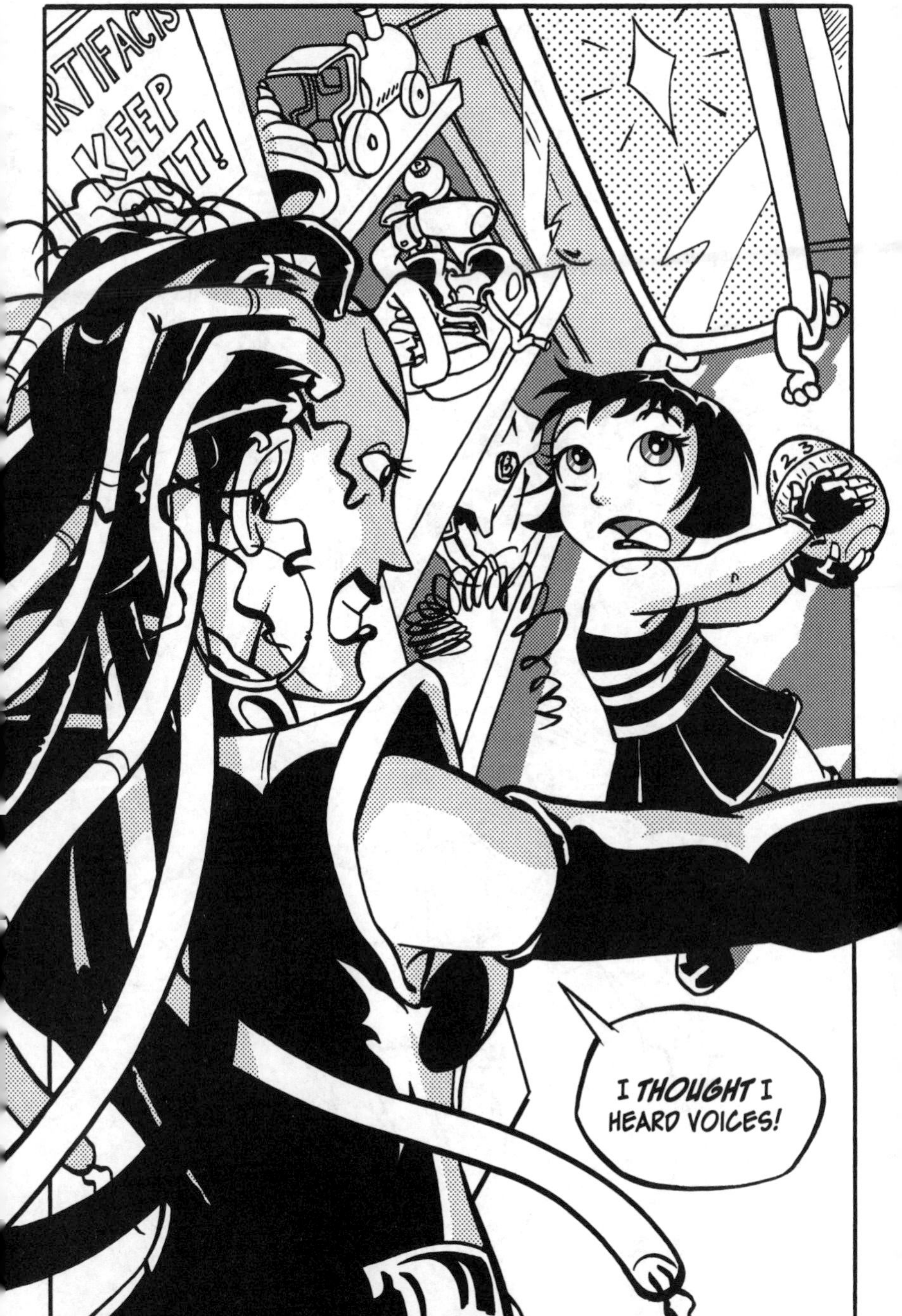
RTIFACTS
KEEP
I *THOUGHT* I HEARD VOICES!

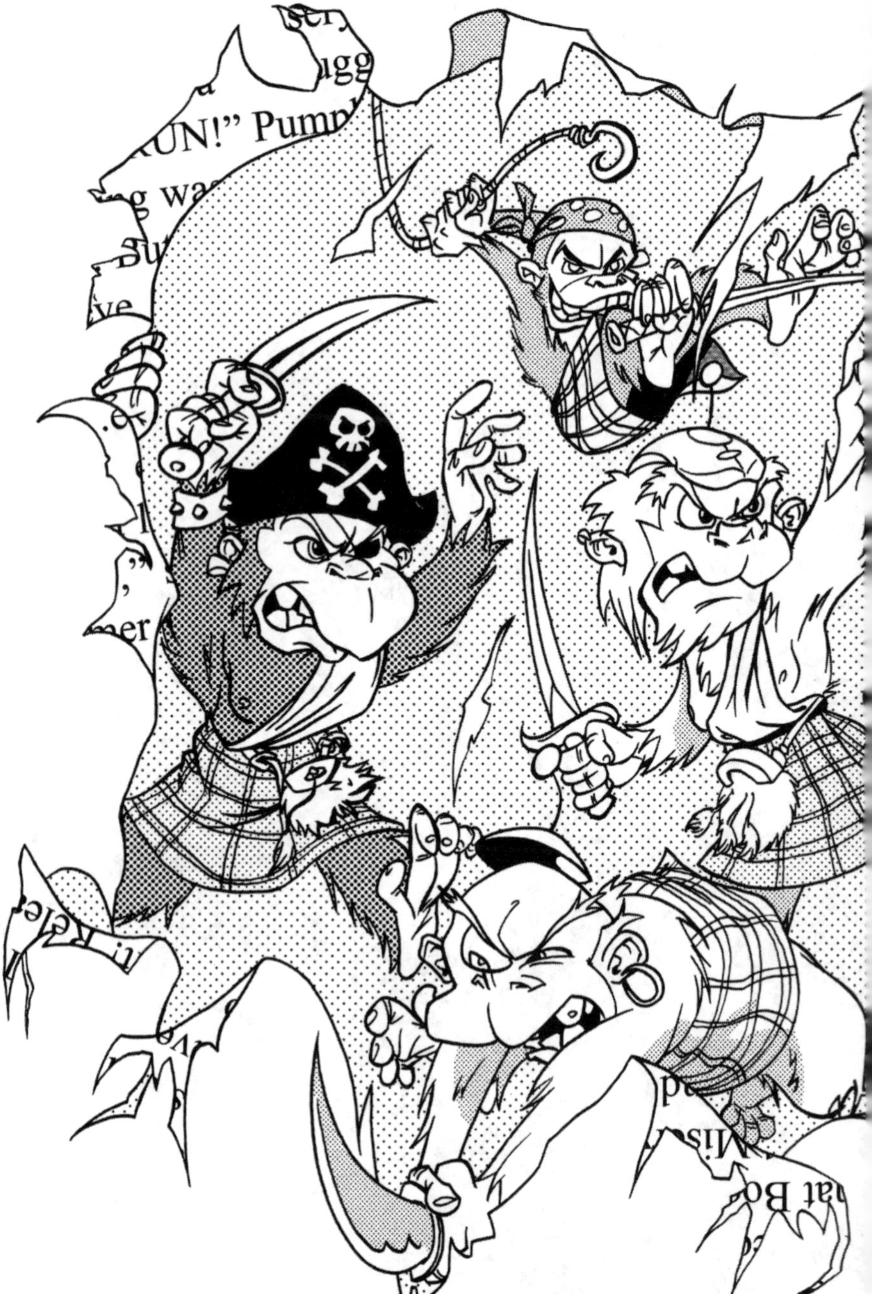

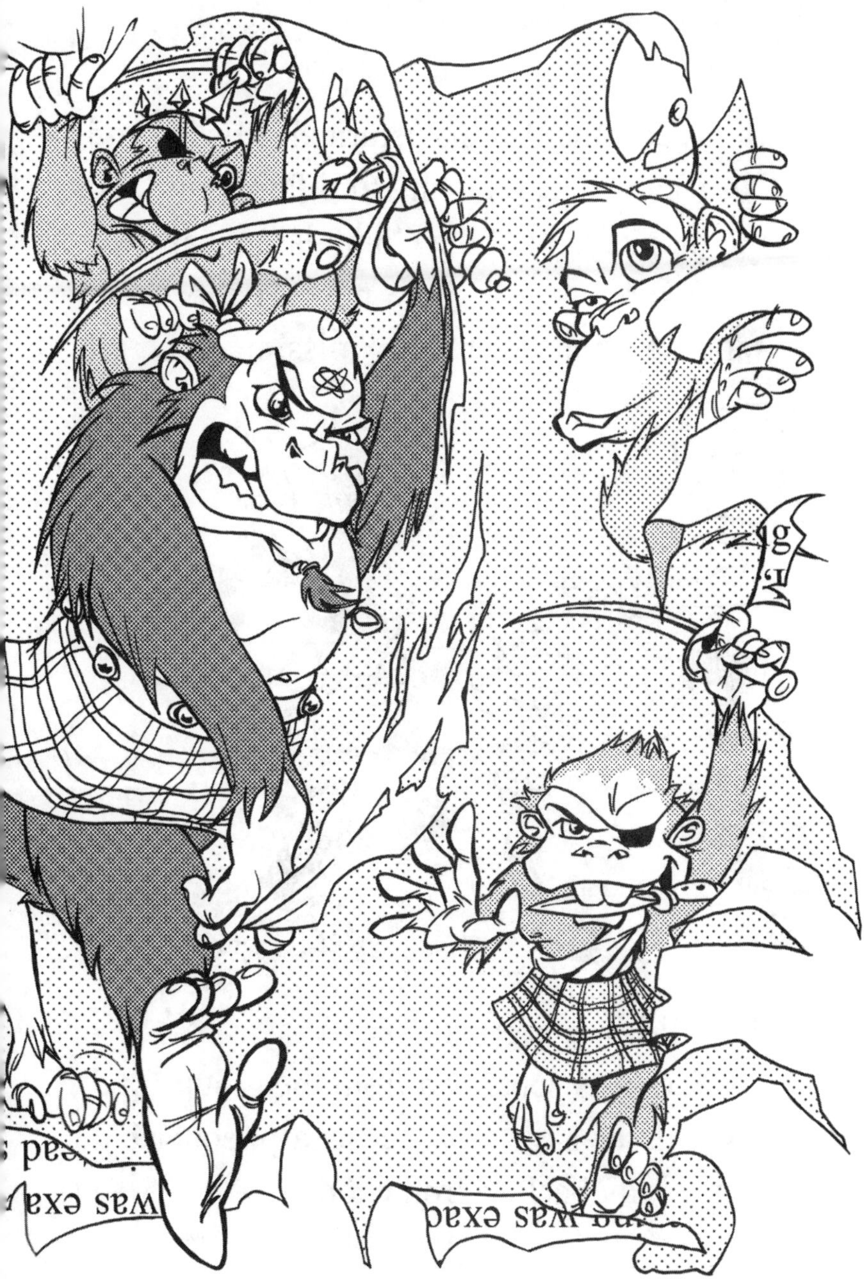

When the Agents returned, Misery and Noir had escaped. But Boo, Pumpkin, and the monkeys held the Commissars captive.

After that, all three new Agents were sent on their first solo mission. But all

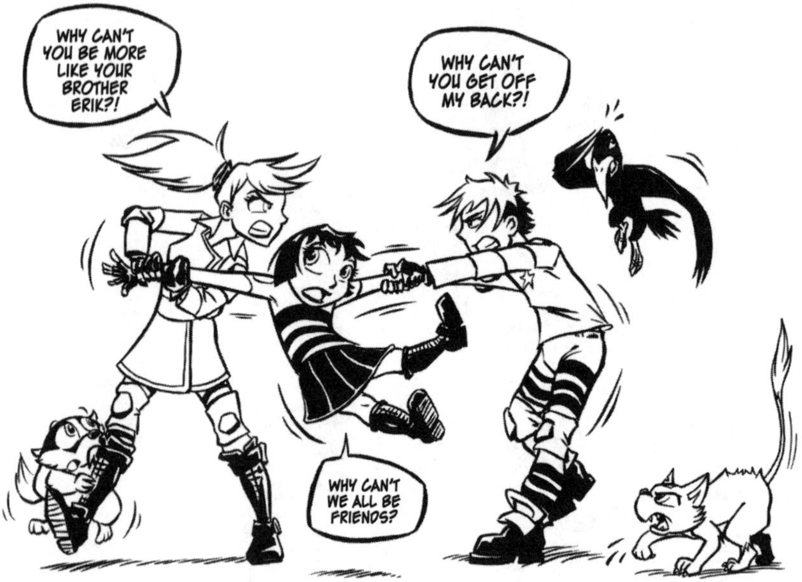
WHY CAN'T YOU BE MORE LIKE YOUR BROTHER ERIK?!
WHY CAN'T YOU GET OFF MY BACK?!
WHY CAN'T WE ALL BE FRIENDS?

they did was argue.

Kira was separated from the group. And Commissar Noir took her as a prisoner but all the way back to Iron City!

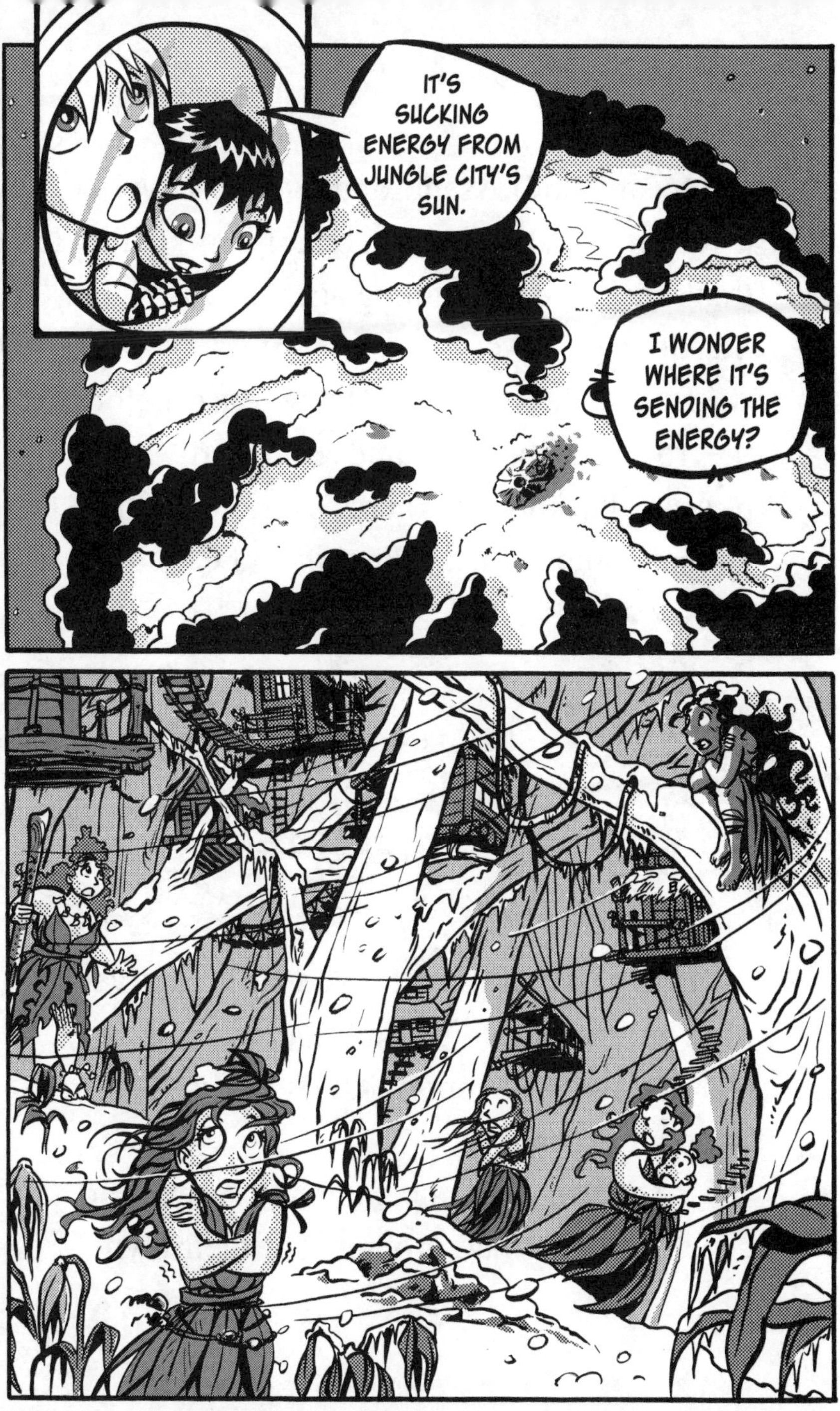
IT'S SUCKING ENERGY FROM JUNGLE CITY'S SUN.
I WONDER WHERE IT'S SENDING THE ENERGY?

Meanwhile, Asano and Boo discovered a rocket crawling with Commissars. Quick thinking helped the young agents destroy the Starflower Rocket.

Boo called back to Home Base before the rocket exploded, and Boo and Asano returned back to the Agents' Aerie with their animal companions, Pumpkin and Quoth.

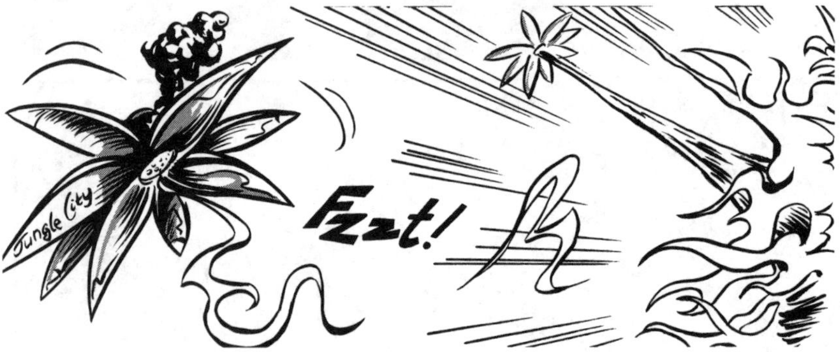
Jungle City
Fzzt!

But Kira and Seeker were still captives of Commissar Noir. And the kids hadn't had a chance to report Kira's status to the Supreme Agent yet.

It seemed as if the Supreme Agent and Chief Recorder had problems of their own!

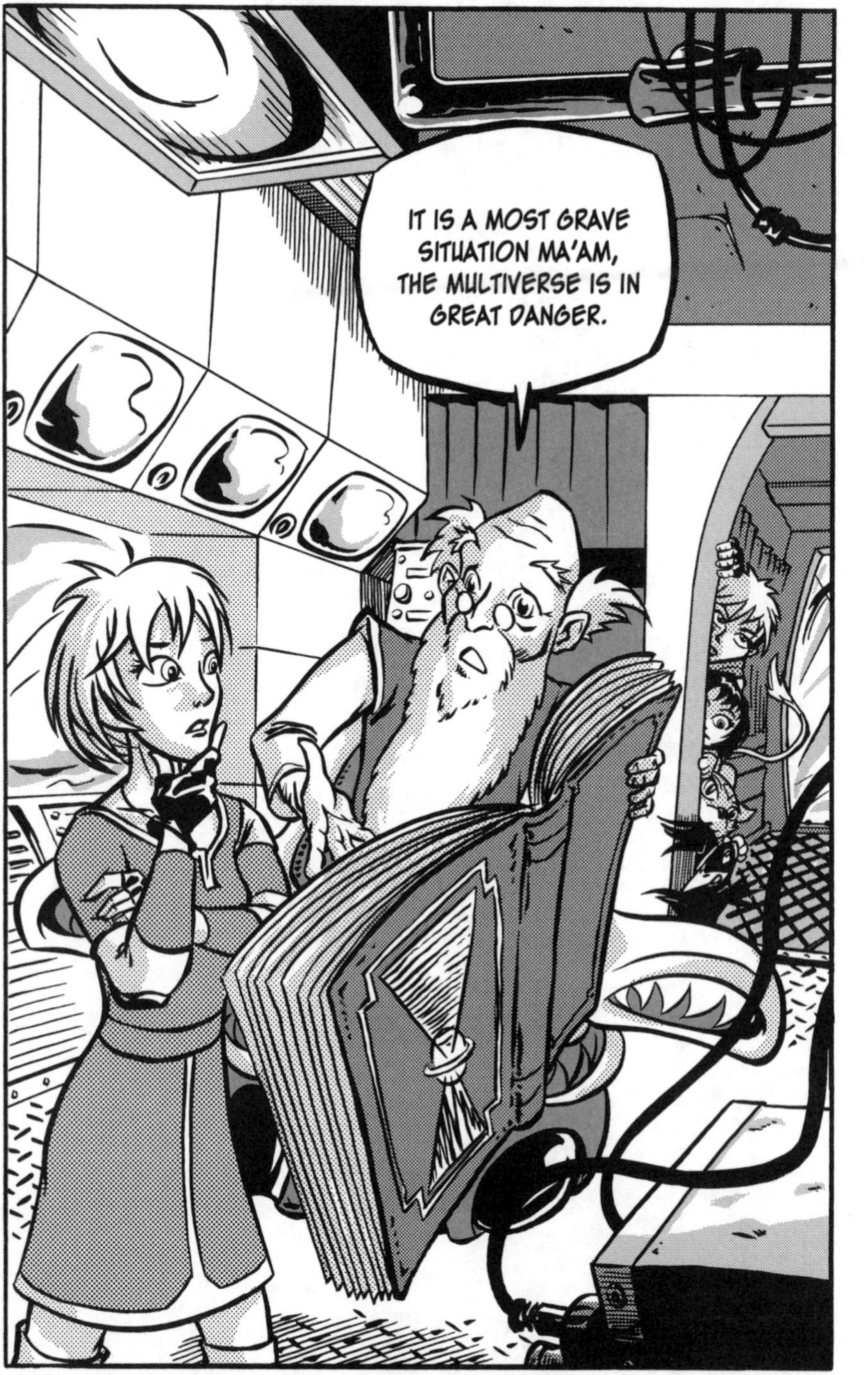
IT IS A MOST GRAVE SITUATION MA'AM, THE MULTIVERSE IS IN GREAT DANGER.

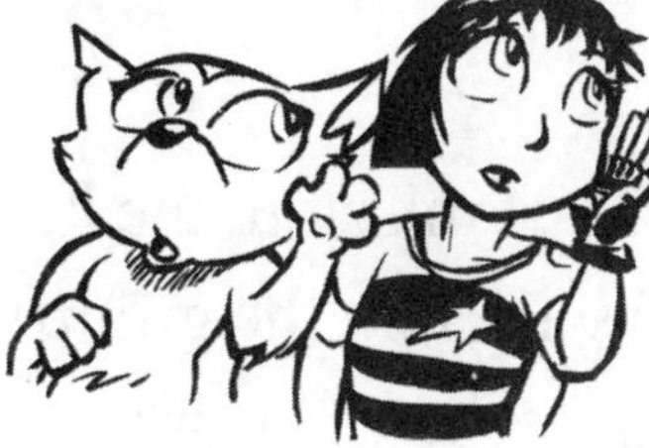

Chapter 2
A Time of Gifts

The Agents waited in the office. Boo sat by the wall. Asano stood next to her. He shifted from foot to foot. Pumpkin and Quoth, their animal companions, kept near. They all hid their eyes.

If only the Supreme Agent and Chief Recorder weren't so busy! All they had to do was look to see what was written on their four faces!

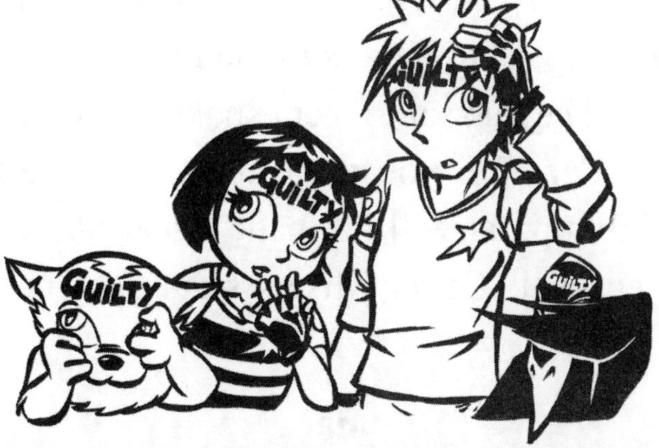
GUILTY
GUILTY
GUILTY
GUILTY

On their last mission, the kids had a fight with Kira. As a result, the group split up. Kira ran off with Seeker, her animal companion. Then she was captured by Queen Misery and Commissar Noir!

The Agents felt bad. They were worried about their friend. They finally had found the courage to tell the Supreme Agent. But the Supreme Agent had worries, too. She had told the Agents to wait!

"What will we tell the Lords Spatial and Temporal?" asked the Supreme Agent. The Chief Recorder dialed a secret number on the control panel.

"When can we tell the Supreme Agent?" asked Asano. "I feel like anything that happens to Kira is my fault!"

The Supreme Agent spoke to the Chief Recorder. "Do you think the Lords Spatial and Temporal will be mad? I feel like I've failed us all. Queen Misery's Starflowers are all over. They're stealing energy from all the suns in the Multiverse!"

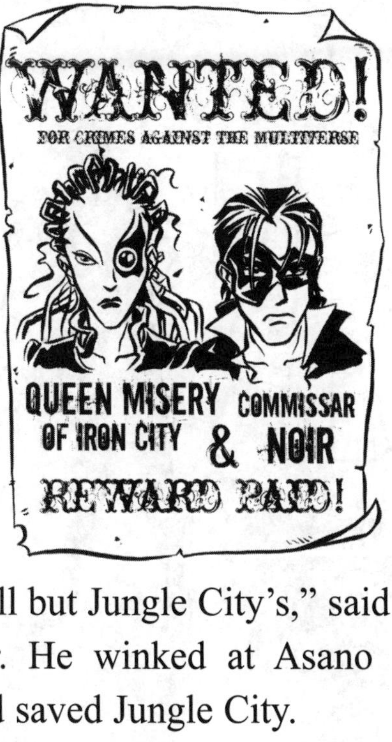
WANTED!
FOR CRIMES AGAINST THE MULTIVERSE
QUEEN MISERY
OF IRON CITY
&
COMMISSAR
NOIR
REWARD PAID!

"All but Jungle City's," said the Chief Recorder. He winked at Asano and Boo. They had saved Jungle City.

"That's right," the Supreme Agent said, but she was still worried. "What will I tell them?"

"Why not the truth?" asked a young voice that sparkled like diamonds might.

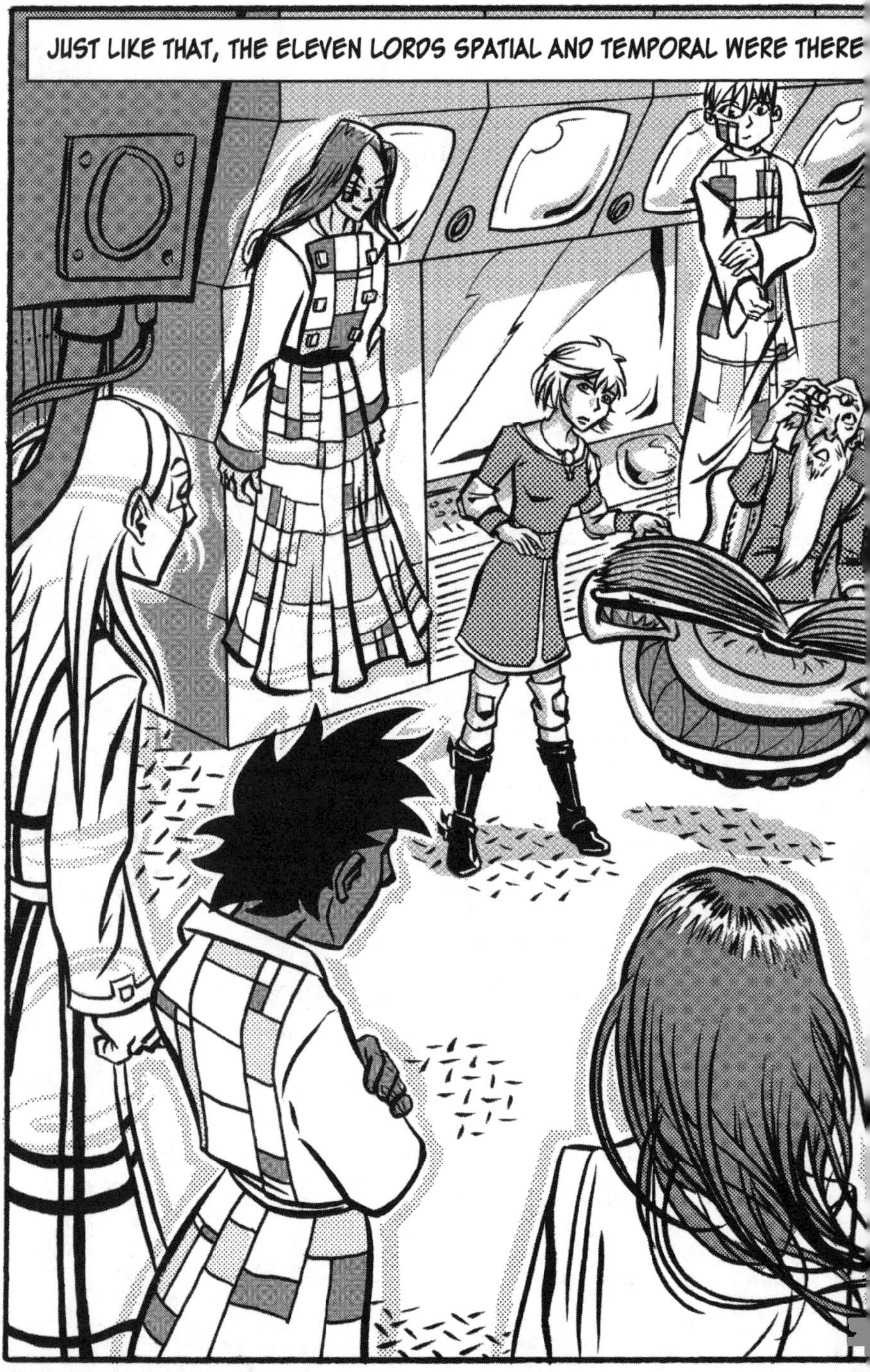
JUST LIKE THAT, THE ELEVEN LORDS SPATIAL AND TEMPORAL WERE THERE

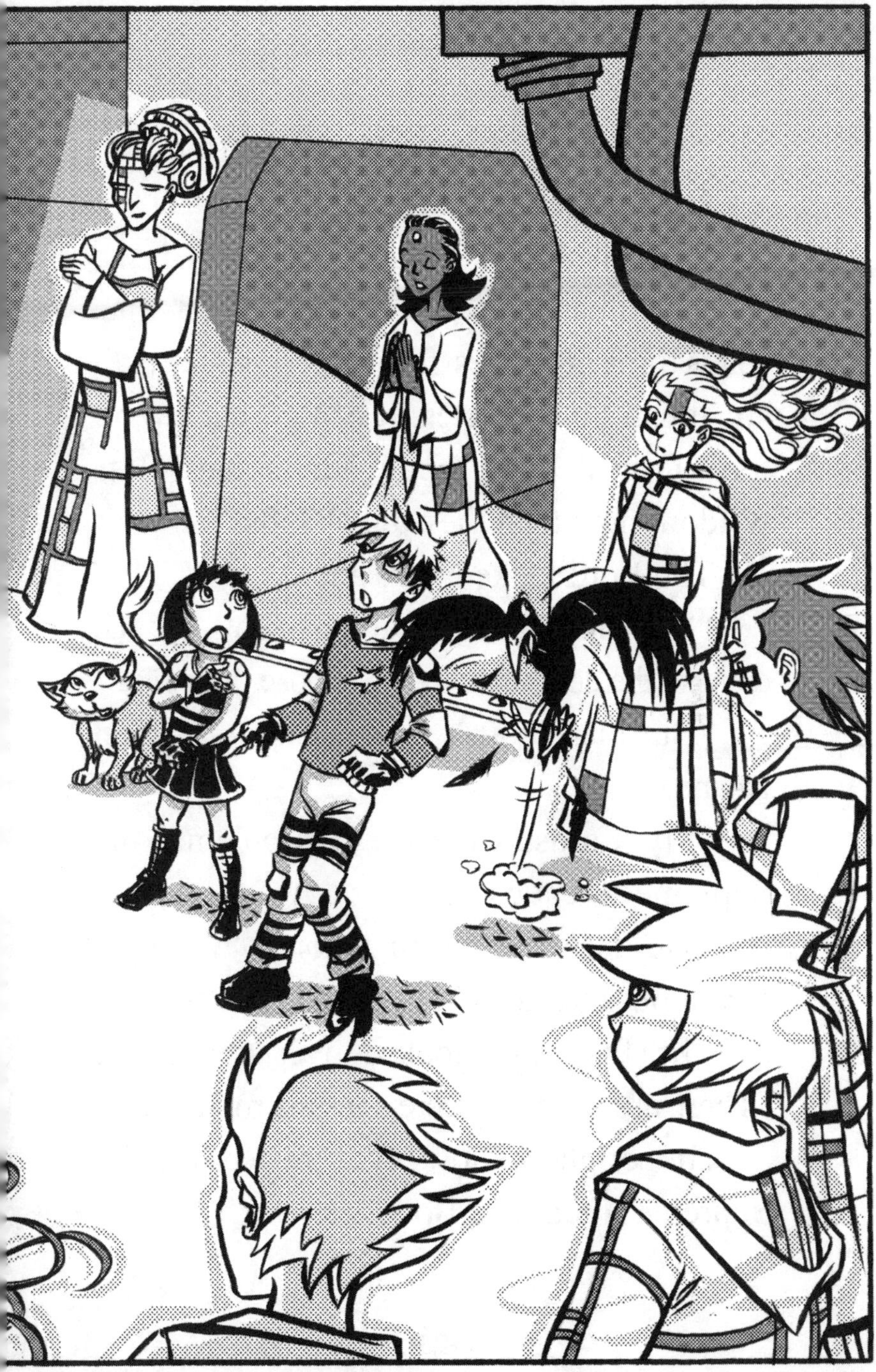

"They look so young!" gasped Boo.

One of the Lords turned to Boo.

"Age isn't the same as wisdom," she said. "Humans see time as a straight line. They think it moves forward. But that isn't so! It can go in circles. It can go backward, too. That is why some adults have less wisdom now than they did as kids!"

The Lord looked at Asano.

"We think of time as a group of dots. We can connect the dots any way we choose," she said.

"But that doesn't make sense—" began Asano.

"My Lords, we have a problem," the Supreme Agent cut in.

"We do," said the first Lord, "when we forget our manners." He gave her a frown.

The first Lord looked over the group. "There are so many secrets in this room. . . ."

His bright yellow eyes rested on the Supreme Agent and Boo.

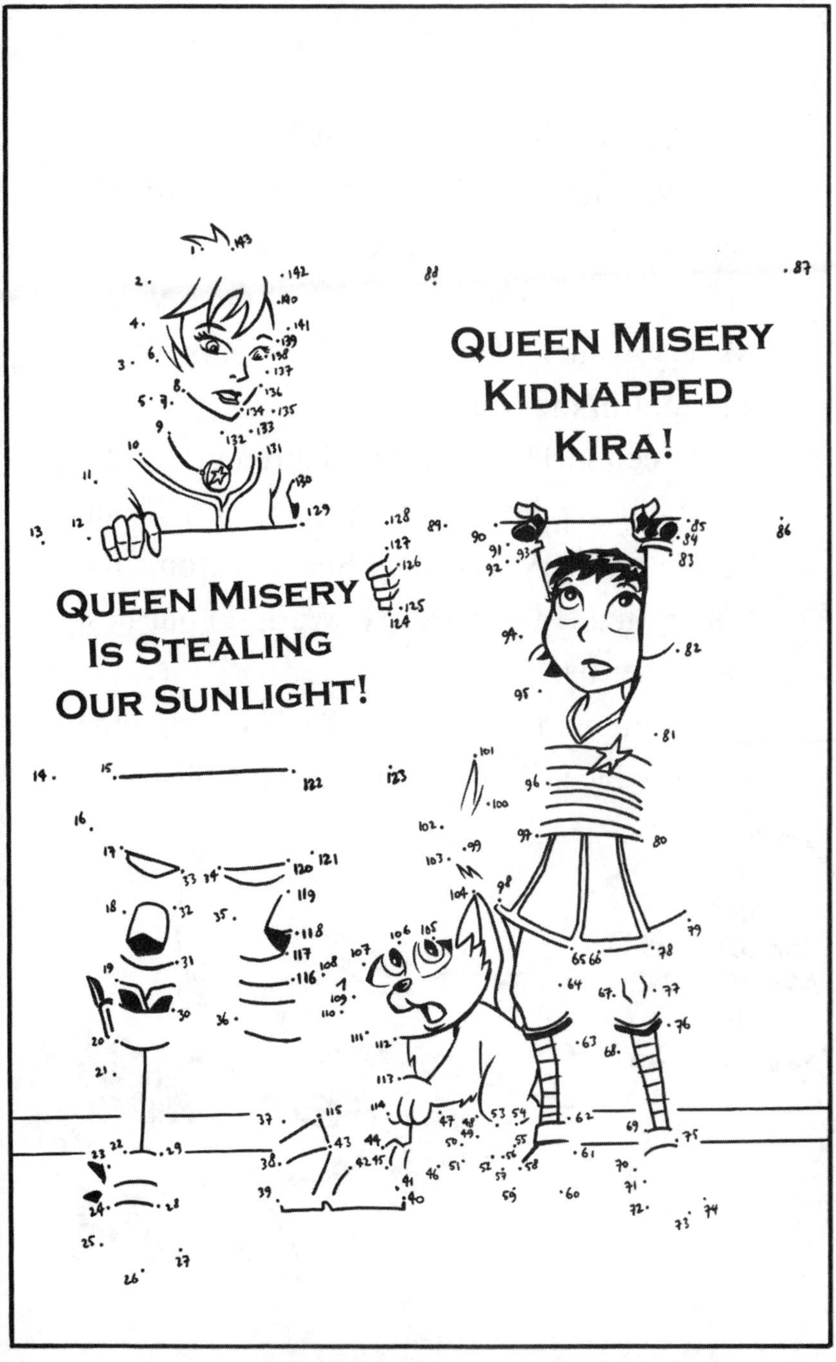
QUEEN MISERY KIDNAPPED KIRA!
QUEEN MISERY IS STEALING OUR SUNLIGHT!

Can you see what he saw?

"My, my, my," said the first Lord. He shook his head. "Queen Misery sure is greedy. A teen girl has a lot of energy. But Misery wants even more. She wants all the sunlight in the Multiverse."

"Teen girl?" asked the Supreme Agent.

Asano couldn't hold it in. He cried out, "Queen Misery has Kira! She's in Iron City. It's my fault! I'm so sorry. We'll do our best to get her back!"

"Kira is in Iron City?" The Supreme Agent's face lit up. "That's great news!"

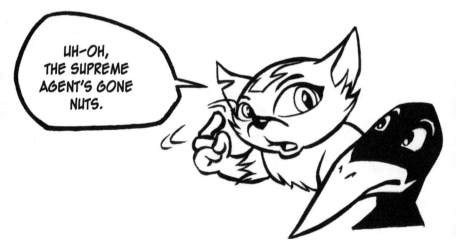

UH-OH, THE SUPREME AGENT'S GONE NUTS.

"What?!" asked the Agents.

"Kids," asked the Chief Recorder, "do you know what makes Iron City special?"

"Sure," said Boo. She always listened in class. "It can change location!"

"Oh yeah!" said Asano. "That's why we can't open a Gate to it!"

"Yes!" said the Chief Recorder. "But we COULD open a Gate to it . . . "

" . . . if there were a signal," said the Supreme Agent.

"Like the one . . . " started Boo.

" . . . on Kira's uniform!" finished Asano.

"HOORAY!" cried the Agents. "We're saved! Now we can invade Iron City and fix our problems!"

"Not quite. You also must think of your enemy's problems," said the second Lord.

"What problems does Queen Misery have?" asked Pumpkin.

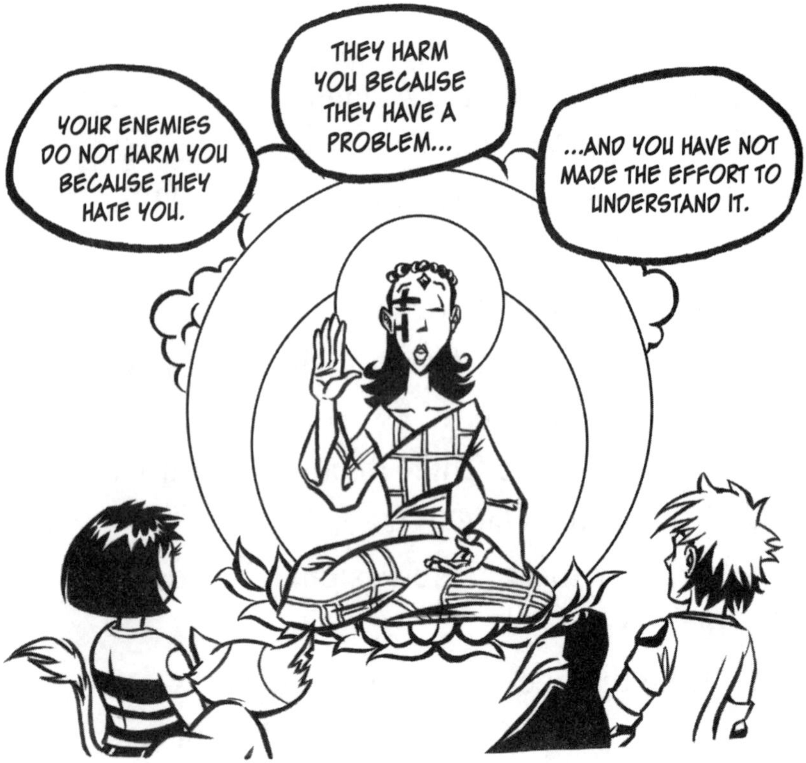
YOUR ENEMIES DO NOT HARM YOU BECAUSE THEY HATE YOU.
THEY HARM YOU BECAUSE THEY HAVE A PROBLEM...
...AND YOU HAVE NOT MADE THE EFFORT TO UNDERSTAND IT.

"And what do they have to do with us?" asked Asano.

"Stars don't live forever," said the first Lord. "Iron City's star will soon take its last fiery breath. Moving around between dimensions drained too much of its energy."

"Is that why Queen Misery is stealing sunlight?" asked Boo. "For her star?"

"Yes, Agent Boo," said the first Lord. He shook his head. "But it won't work."

"Not even we can keep the star alive," said the first Lord. "The Starflowers can't save Iron City. But they can destroy the other worlds."

"We've been taking out as many as we can," said the Supreme Agent. "Now we can send a team of Agents to Iron City. And we can try to help Misery with her problem."

The second Lord smiled. "When you pick your team, think small," she said, looking at Boo.

"Oh, Boo and Asano are just starting out," said the Supreme Agent.

"But they are lucky," said the first Lord. "And we have something to help."

"We left it here the last time we visited you," said the second Lord.

"Yes, it's under the seat," said the first Lord.

"What?" asked the Chief Recorder. "Oof! That's why this chair is so bumpy!"

He pulled out an object from under the cushion.

"Can I see?" asked Asano.

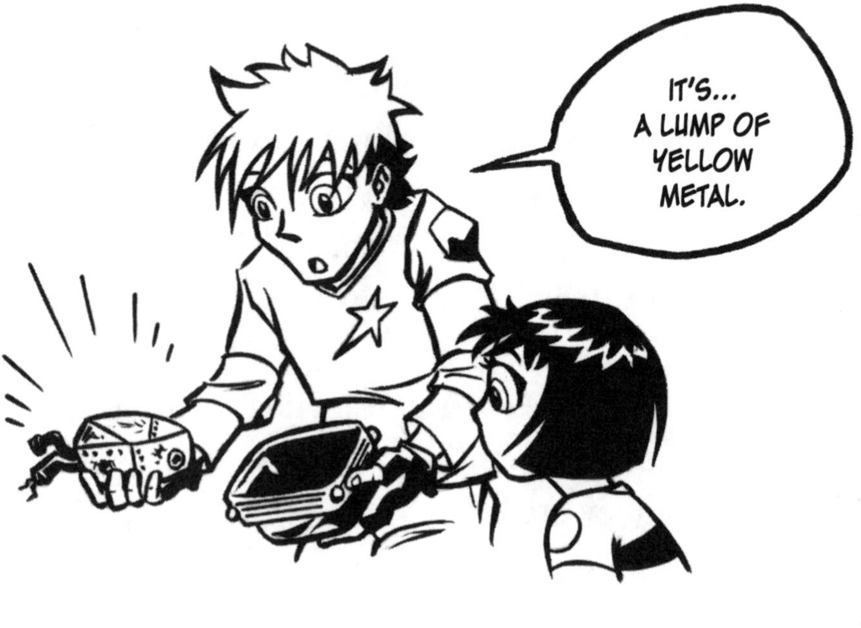
IT'S... A LUMP OF YELLOW METAL.

"What is it?" Boo asked.

Boo could see through the first Lord. He was turning into mist!

He answered her in a fading voice. "It's an Artifact. You'll find out what it does when you need it."

Asano tossed the lump from hand to hand. "It would make a good slamball. . . ."

Boo waved her hands. "No! I don't think that's a good idea!"

"Are the Lords Spatial and Temporal always so puzzling?" Asano asked.

"Every single time," said the Chief Recorder.

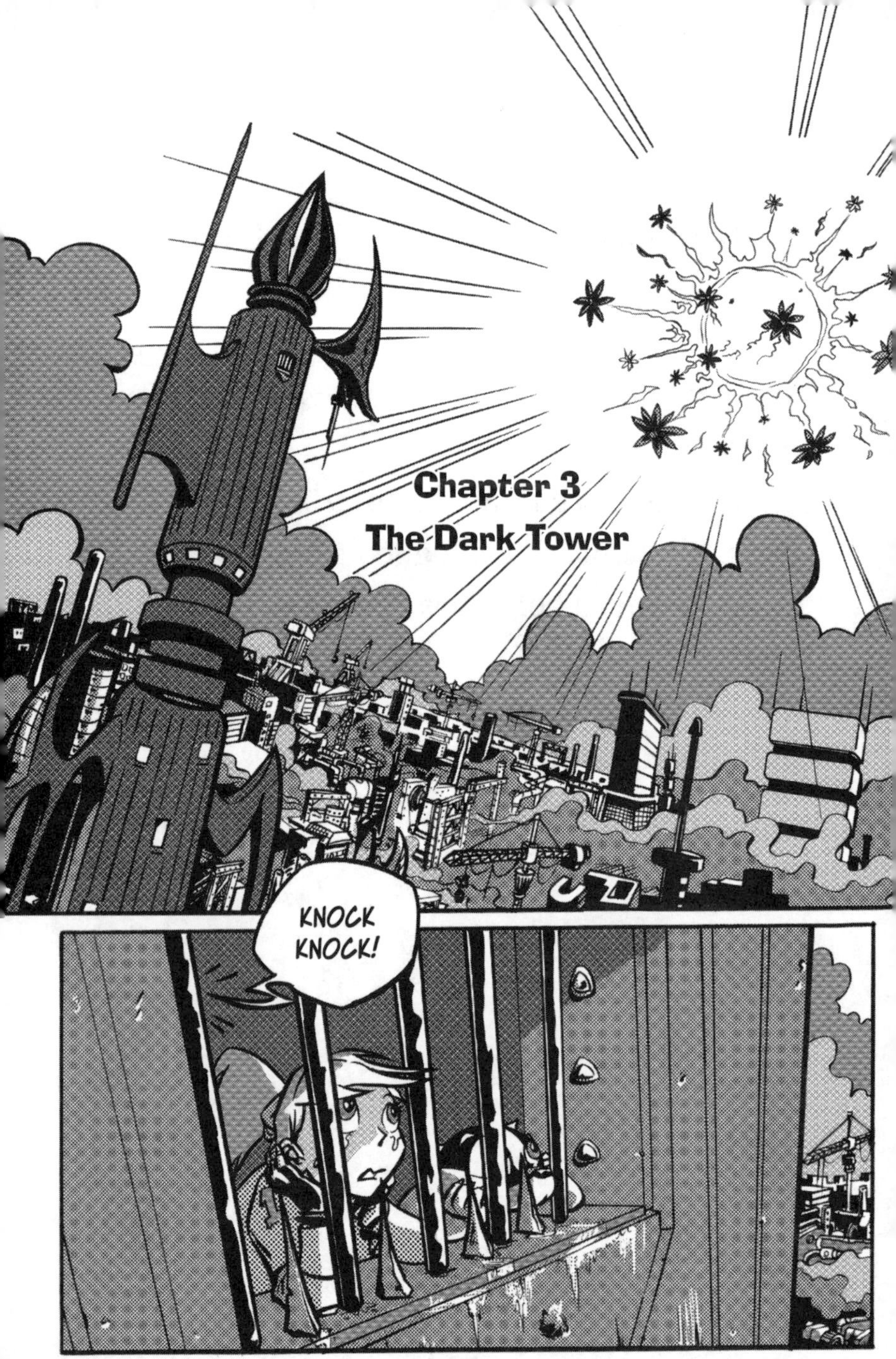
Chapter 3
The Dark Tower
KNOCK KNOCK!

"Go away!" Kira said. She didn't turn. She knew what she would see. It would be Commissar Noir, the ex-Agent who had captured her.

"I have food for you. You haven't eaten all day," he said.

"I'm not hungry!" Kira shot back. She didn't want to take her eyes off the sky. Teams of Agents were working hard. And Kira could see the result. She watched the Starflowers around Iron City's sun die, one by one.

Kira focused. She hoped her willpower could help the Agents.

"I've got ice cream sundaes, too," said Noir. "I'll give you the chocolate one."

Kira turned with anger. "Do you think I can be bought off with ice cream? That after one taste I'll shout, 'Yes! Sign me up for your evil plan! I want to stay here in ugly old Iron City!'?"

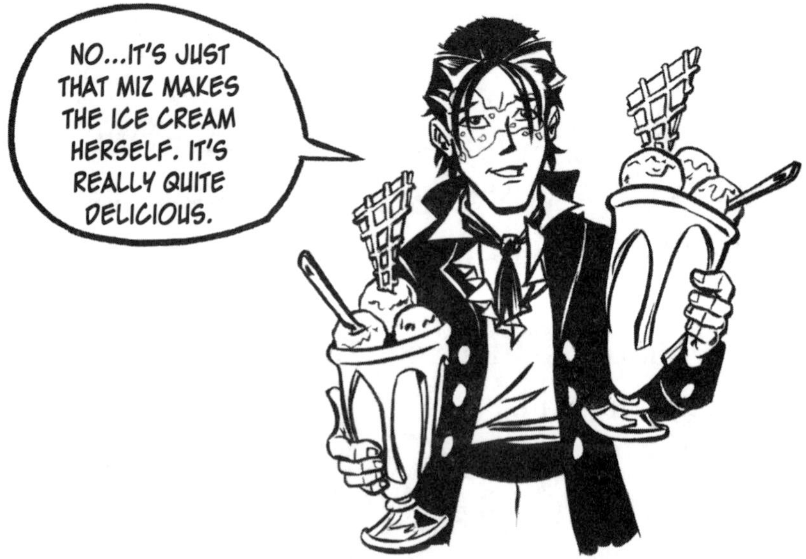
NO...IT'S JUST THAT MIZ MAKES THE ICE CREAM HERSELF. IT'S REALLY QUITE DELICIOUS.

"'"Miz?!"'" asked Kira.

"To her friends," said Noir.

"And HOW MANY of those are there?" asked Kira.

"Um . . . " said Noir.

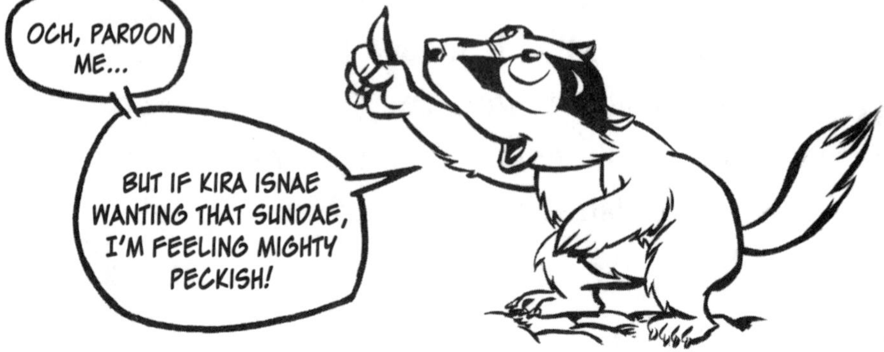
OCH, PARDON ME...
BUT IF KIRA ISNAE WANTING THAT SUNDAE, I'M FEELING MIGHTY PECKISH!

"I'll take it," said Kira. "But first . . . I want to know something. Why did you give up being an Agent? And why do you work for our enemy?"

"Can I just give you the vanilla sundae instead?" asked Noir. "Then you'll feel like you haven't given in, and I don't have to answer."

"Or maybe we could get a third sundae for the animal," said Seeker. "I like strawberry."

"Nope," Kira said, holding out her hand. "Hand over the chocolate."

"Drat," said Seeker.

Noir passed her the sundae.

"This is good!" Kira said, her mouth full.

"Yes," said Noir. He took a bite of the vanilla. "It's never too sweet."

They ate their ice cream in silence. Then Noir said, "I'm not hungry. Seeker, would you finish this?"

Noir turned to Kira. "You're just starting out as an Agent. So it seems new and fun, doesn't it?"

Kira nodded.

"You feel like you're doing something really good, yes?"

Kira nodded.

"After twenty years, you'll wish people would just STAY saved."

"That's not nice!" said Kira.

"But that's how it is. You save a Parallel five, six times . . . then you have to save it again. But when an Agent needs help, where are the people he saved? 'Oh, I might get hurt! It isn't my job!' Or 'I can't stop to help. I have to go meet my friends!'"

"That's not true," said Kira.

"Who has tried to rescue you?" Noir asked. "The Jungle City girls you helped? The other Agents? Who, Agent Kira? Who helps the helpers?"

"That's so sad!" Kira said. "No wonder Queen Misery is your best friend!"

"I'm sorry," said Noir. "I don't mean to upset you. But go easy on Miz. This city is her life. She's given up a lot to save it."

SEE, THE MADRASSA GOT HER, TOO.

Kira thought back to her lessons. "We learned in class that the Madrassa Incident was really bad. But no one ever told us what happened!"

"They wouldn't, would they?" Noir answered.

He stood up and gave Kira his arm. "Come for a walk with me. I'll tell you about the Madrassa Incident. That way I can show you the sights. We may not have much time left to see them, you know."

Kira turned up her nose. "Sights? This ugly place has stuff to see?"

"Iron City isn't ugly," Noir said. "It's just a different kind of beautiful. Let me show you."

Kira's eyes narrowed. Was this a trick?

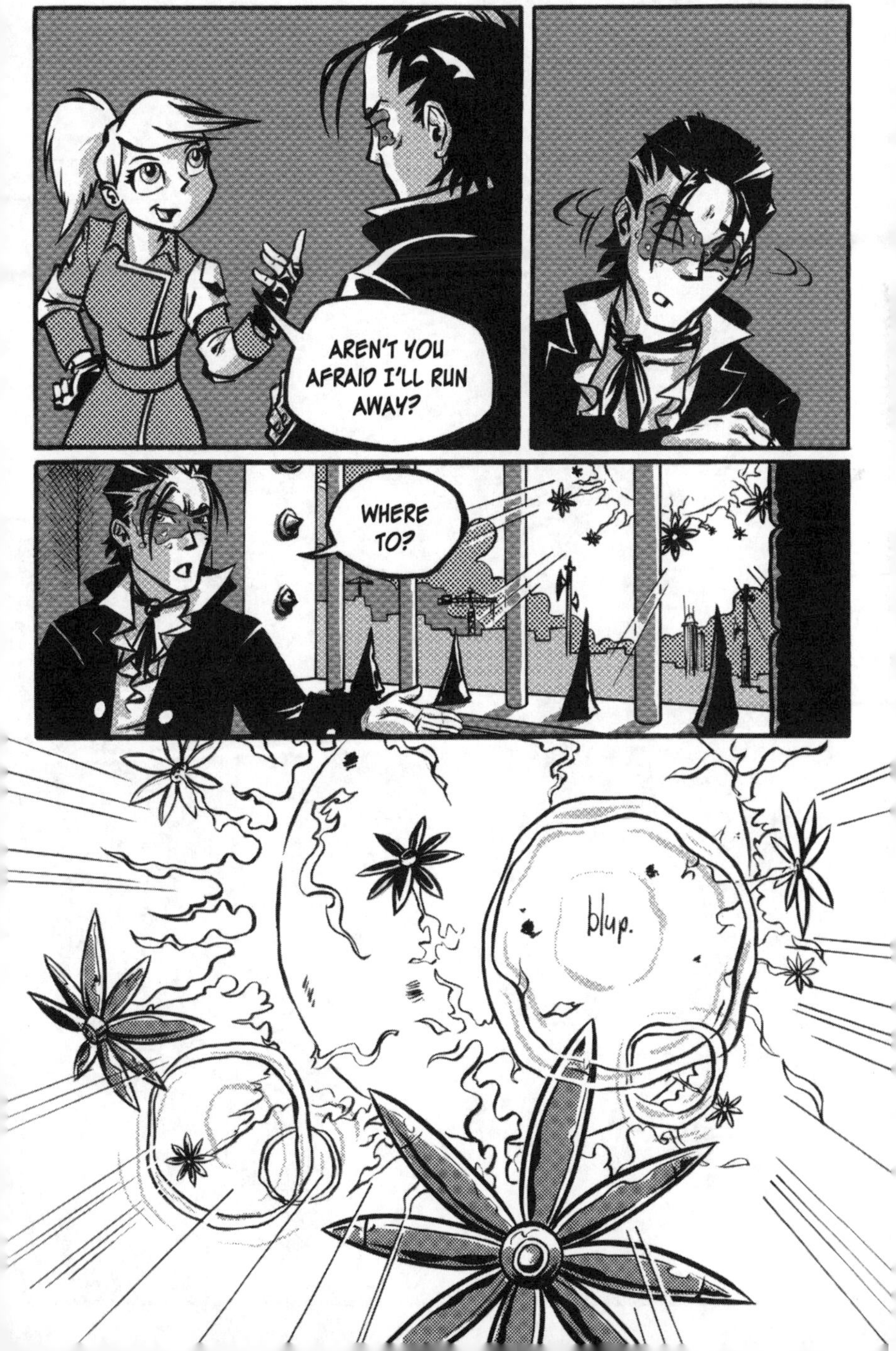
AREN'T YOU AFRAID I'LL RUN AWAY?
WHERE TO?
blup.

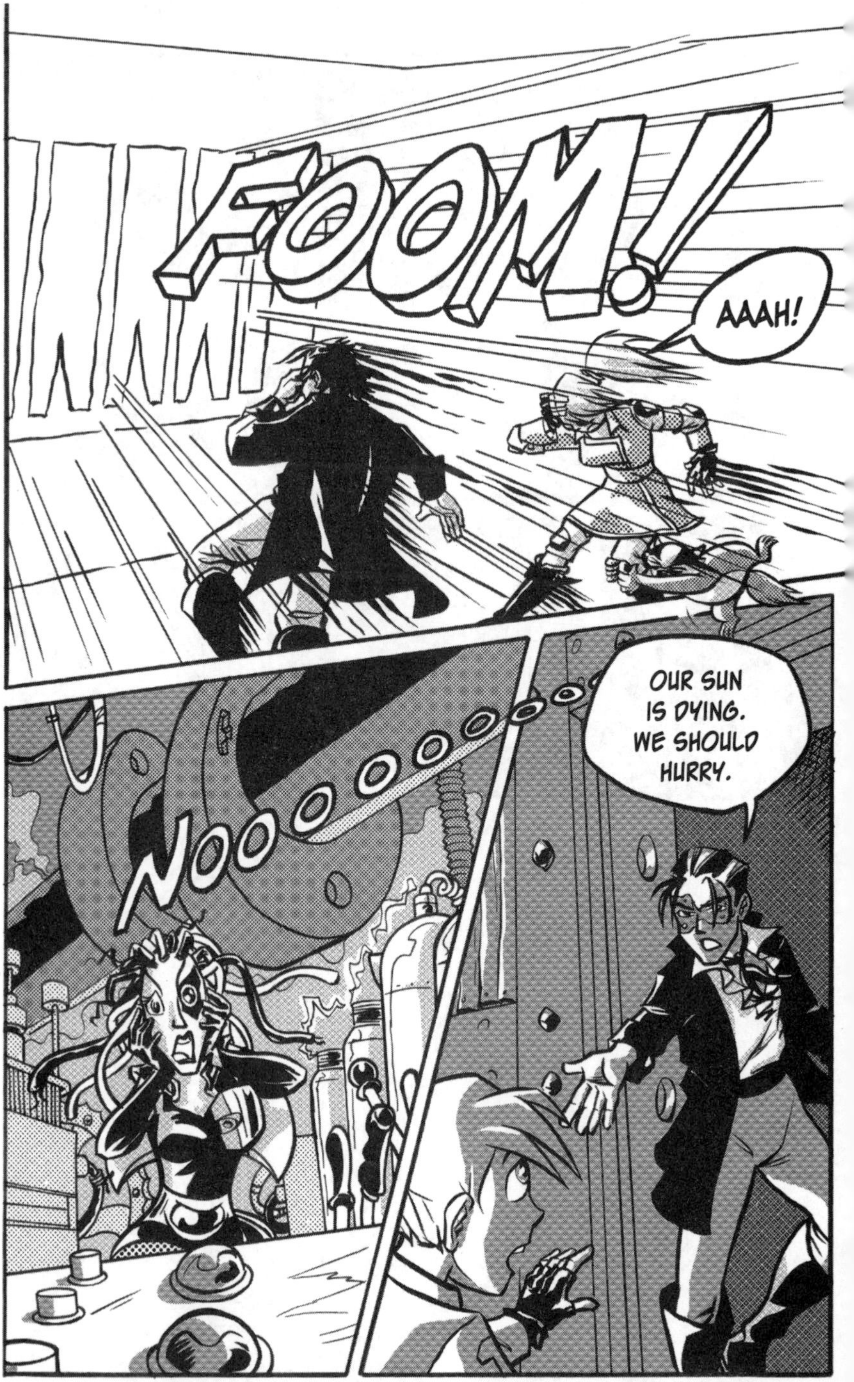
FOOM!
AAAH!
NOOOOOOOOOOOO
OUR SUN IS DYING. WE SHOULD HURRY.

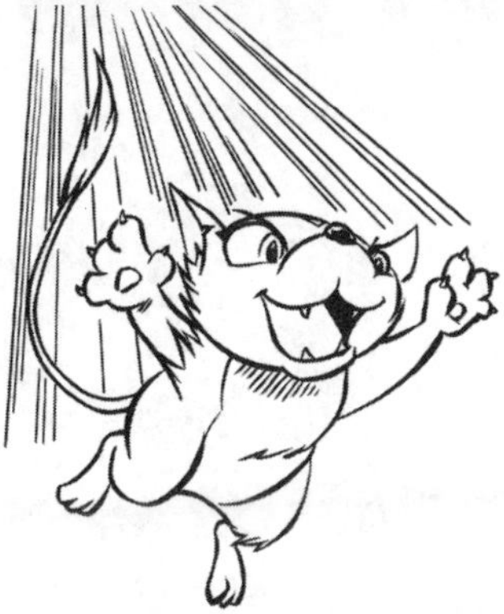

Chapter 4
A Wild Badger Chase

At the edge of Iron City, there was a small sparkle. It grew into an opening. Then, with a big "OUCH!" Boo fell out of the Gate from Space City. She landed right on her rear end!

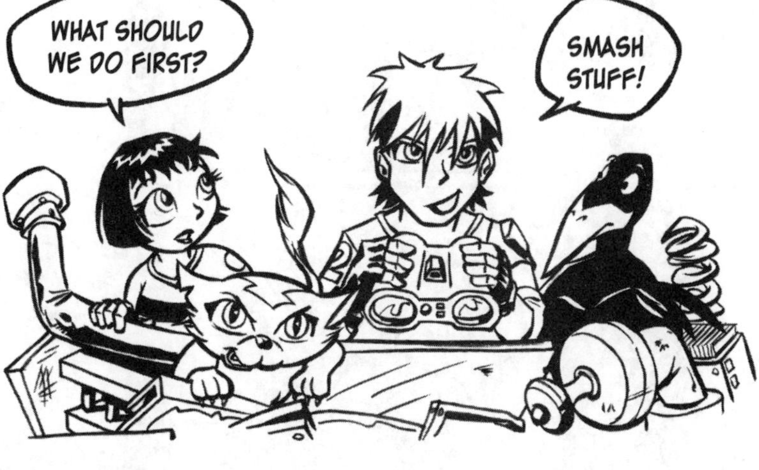
WHAT SHOULD WE DO FIRST?
SMASH STUFF!

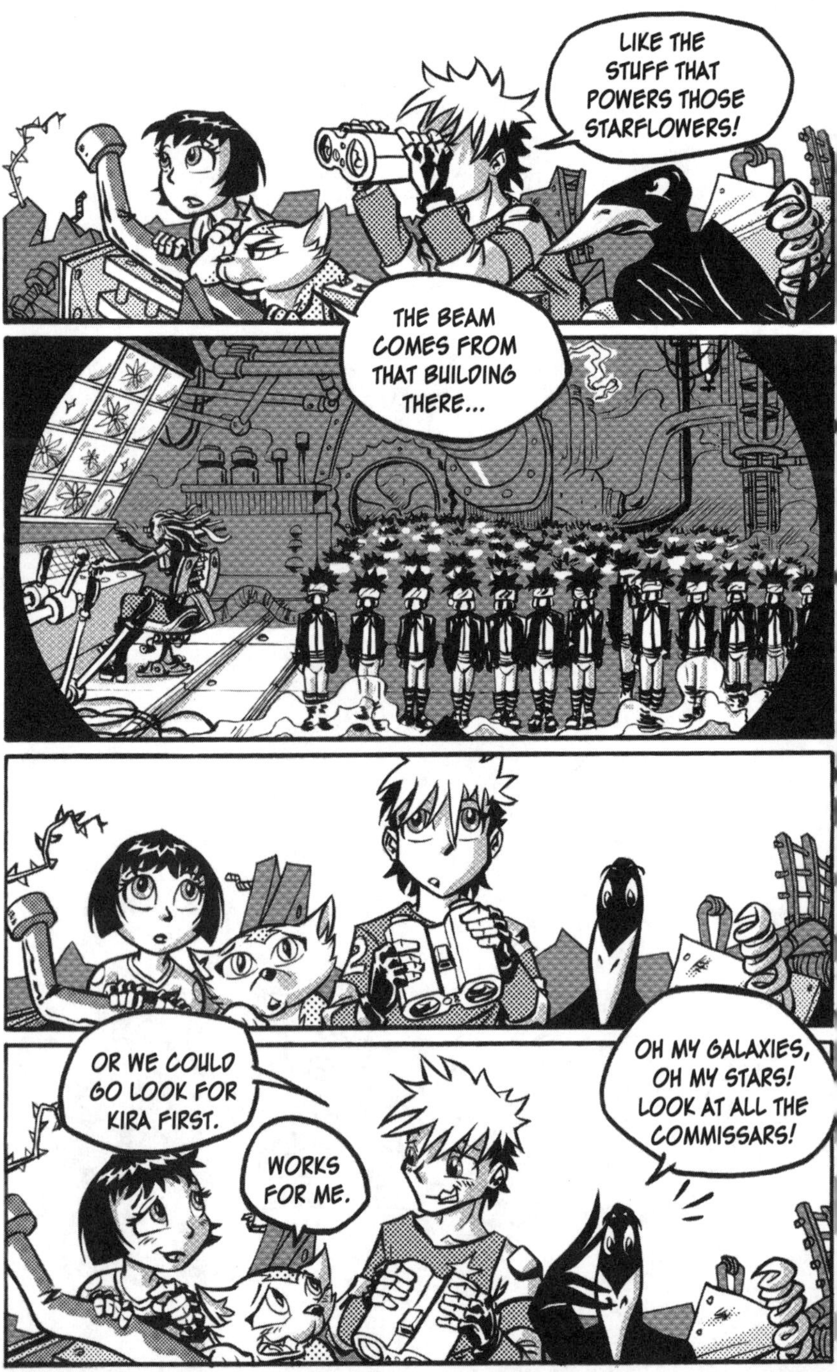
LIKE THE STUFF THAT POWERS THOSE STARFLOWERS!
THE BEAM COMES FROM THAT BUILDING THERE...
OR WE COULD GO LOOK FOR KIRA FIRST.
WORKS FOR ME.
OH MY GALAXIES, OH MY STARS! LOOK AT ALL THE COMMISSARS!

Boo took the lump of metal the Lords Spatial and Temporal had given them from her pocket.

"Maybe the Artifact can help," she said. She cleaned off some of its dirt with her shirt. Boo thought that the Artifact got brighter.

"Oh, Artifact," she said to it, "please show us where Kira is!"

But the lump of metal was silent.

"Just a hint?" Boo asked. She shook the Artifact. "Pretty please?"

"Shh!" Pumpkin said. "Someone is coming."

The kids ducked behind a rock. Two Commissars passed by.

"Forget the Artifact," Asano whispered. "Pumpkin, you got any 'Hot Ginger Death from Above' in stock?"

"Got a fresh batch in this morning," said the cat.

"Then it's Agents away!" shouted Asano, jumping over the rock.

"Wait for me!" said Boo. "I'm coming, too!" Boo climbed over the rock. But Asano and Pumpkin already had tied up the Commissars.

"Tell us where Kira is!" yelled Asano.

"Never," said one of the Commissars.

"Tell us OR ELSE," said Pumpkin.

"Or else what?" asked the other Commissar. "There's nothing you could do to make us tell you our secrets."

"Yeah, we're big and tough," said the first Commissar.

"Bet I can crack them in five minutes," said Pumpkin.

"You're on," said Asano. "What are you going to do?"

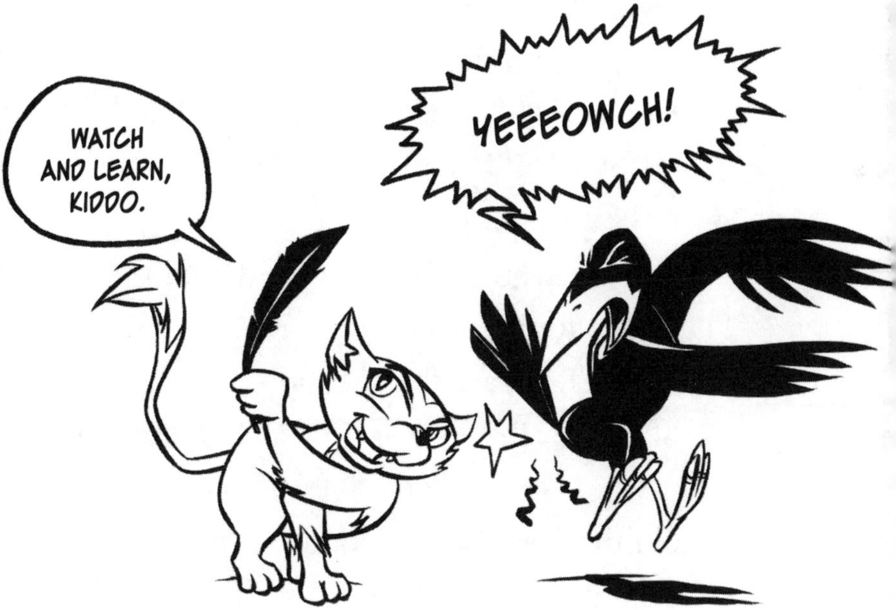
WATCH AND LEARN, KIDDO.
YEEEEOWCH!

"Snort," said the first Commissar.

"Snicker," said the second.

Pumpkin kept tickling.

Asano looked at his watch. "Fifty seconds left," he said.

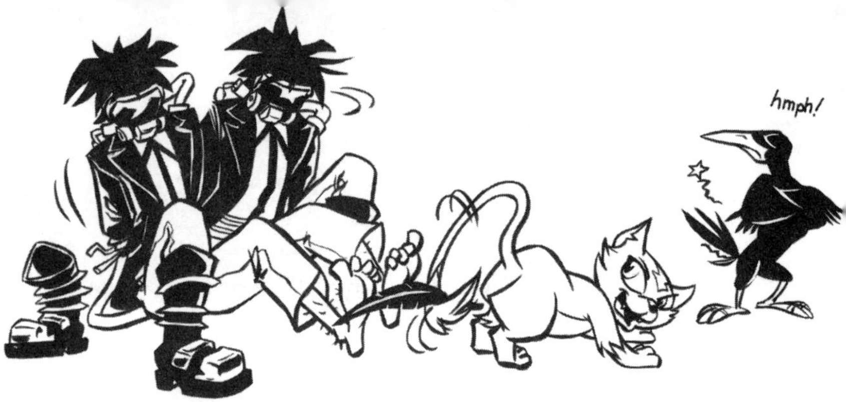
hmph!

"Gulp," said the first Commissar.

"Hee hee HA HA!" said the second.

"STOOOOP!" cried the first. "I can't stand it!"

"Tell us where Kira is," said Pumpkin. "Then I'll stop!"

"NEVER!" said the second.

"She's in the tallest tower!" cried the first.

"Quitter," said the second.

"Shut up," said the first. "At least the cat will stop now."

"I will," said Pumpkin, "but there is one last thing we need from you. . . ."

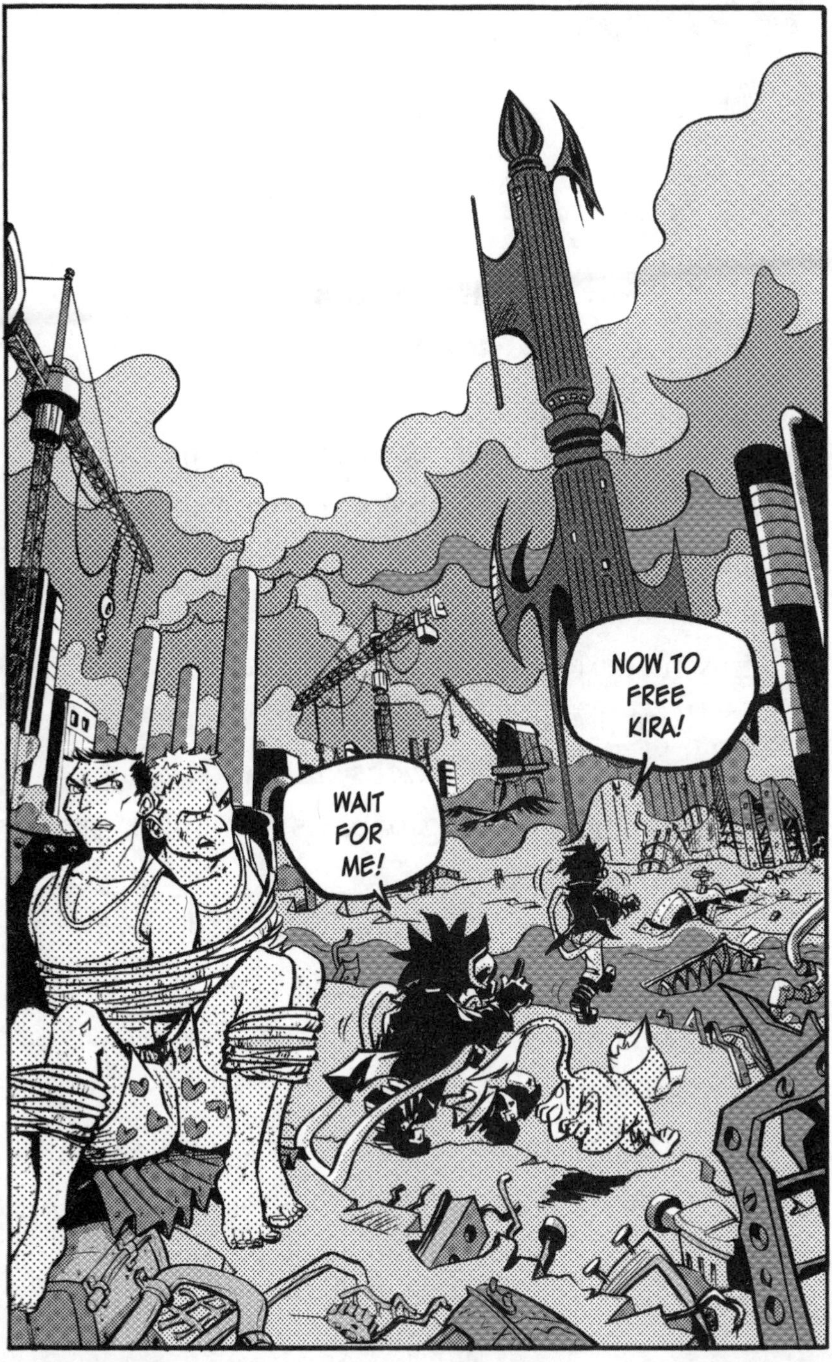
NOW TO FREE KIRA!
WAIT FOR ME!

CHAPTER 5
The Number Garden

"And over there you can see the nests where the Spinnsters weave," Noir said. He pointed at what looked like a metal tower. From inside, Kira could hear a sound like tiny metal feet tapping in impatience.

Kira looked at the tower. There were millions of spider webs inside. A black shadow moved along one. Its hundred eyes all flashed green.

"Ew!" Kira said. She missed the soft, curving shapes of Space City.

Seeker jumped into her arms. "Spiders! I cannae stand spiders!"

"The Spinnsters take getting used to," Noir said. "Come over here to see the

Mother Board. She's the largest computer in the Multiverse."

"Is everything here useful?" asked Kira.

"What?" asked Noir.

"Everything you've shown me makes or does something," Kira answered. "The best parts of a city don't *do* anything. They're just fun . . . or pretty. Isn't there anything here like that?"

"No . . . well, yes, but . . . " Noir blushed.

"Great!" Kira said. "Let's go see it."

"I don't know. You may just say 'Ew!' again," Noir said, walking toward a large junk pile. "You're hard to please."

"Och, tell me about it," said Seeker.

"Or you have a very ugly city," Kira said.

Noir led Kira to a high wall behind the junk pile. It had a small, child-sized door. Noir took a key from his pocket to open it. He bent down and stepped through. Kira followed.

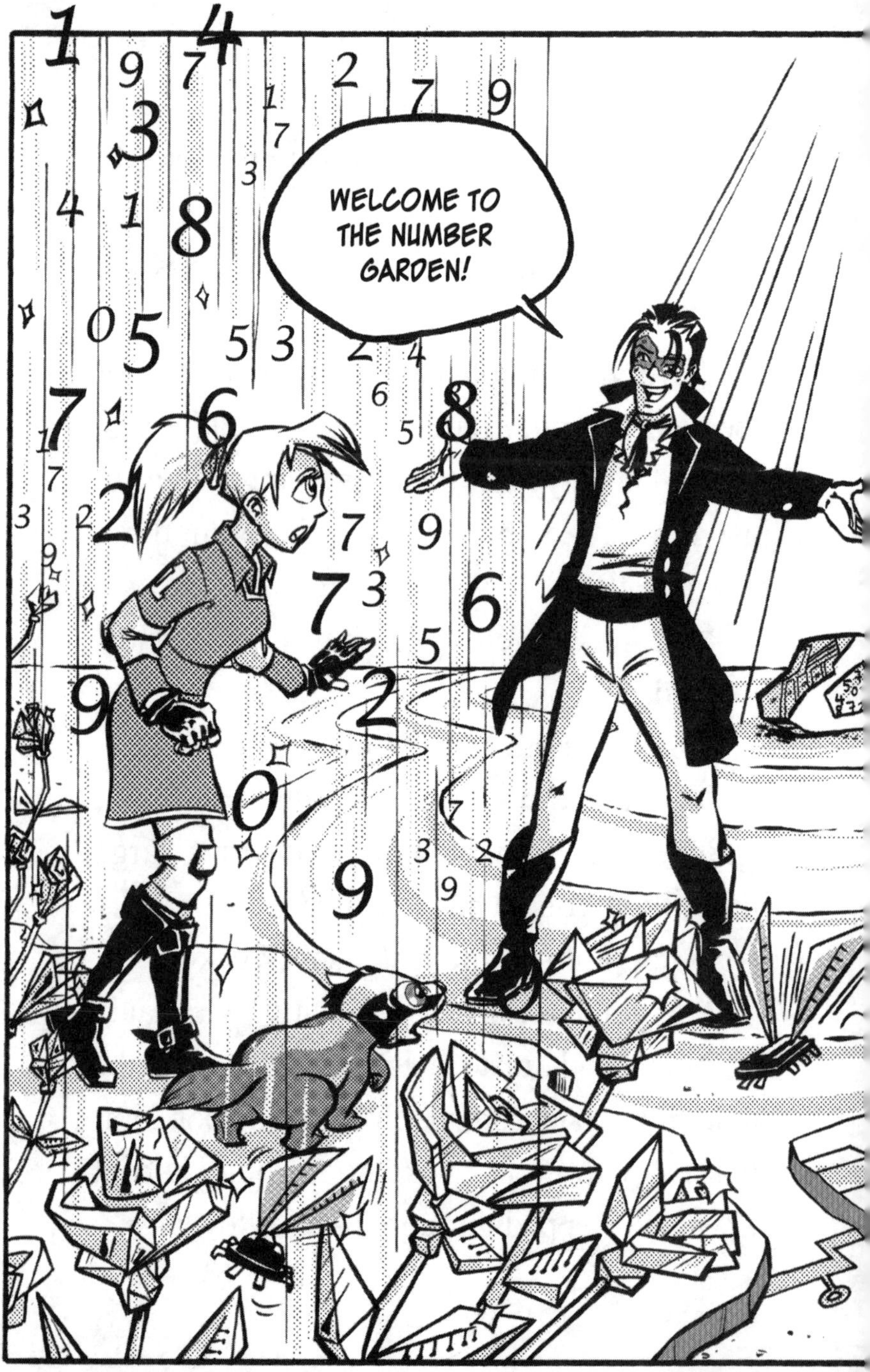
WELCOME TO THE NUMBER GARDEN!

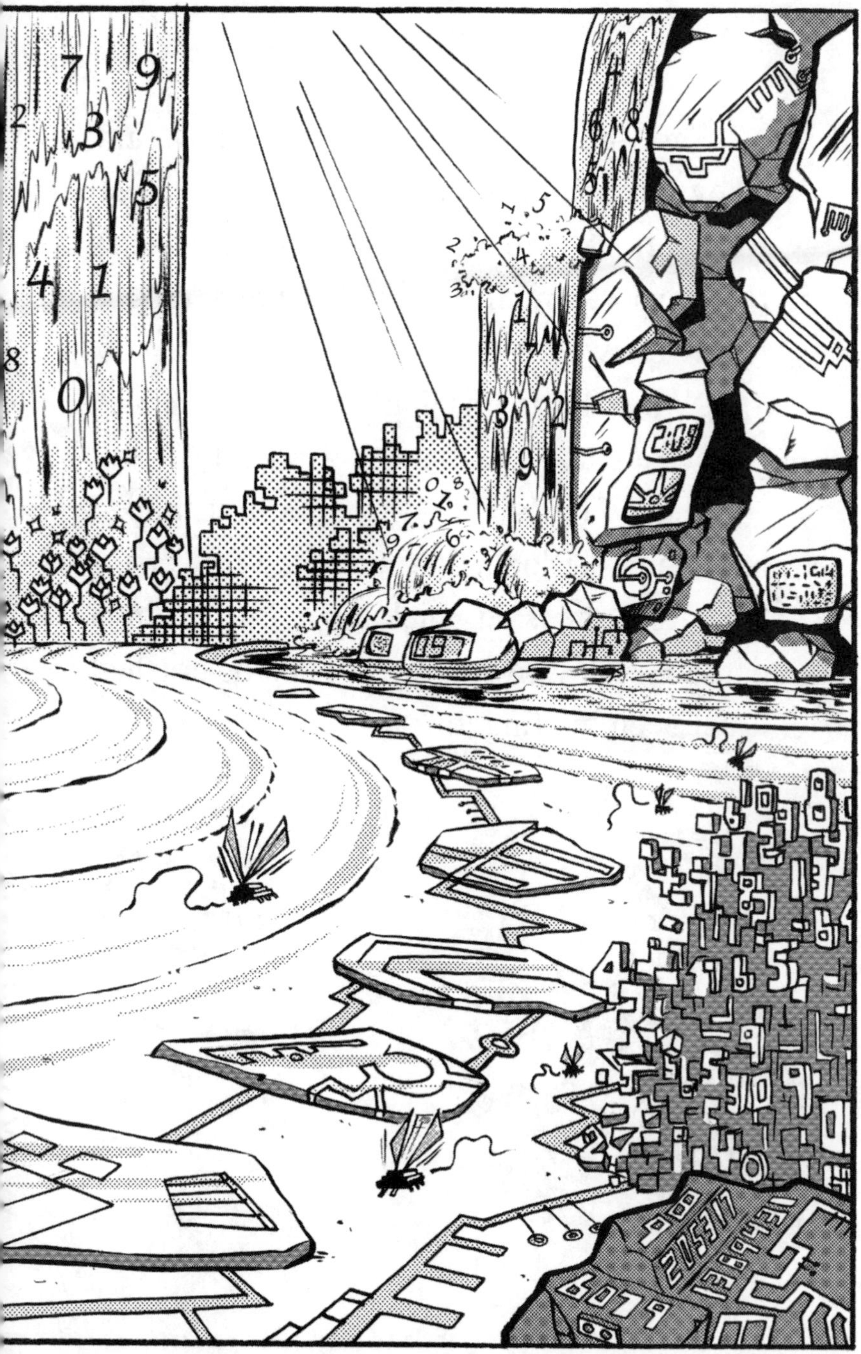

Kira gasped. Numbers fell like rain. They dropped to the sand where crystal roses grew. Metal flowers covered dark rock. And a small ocean of pebbles moved in perfect waves.

"Wow, this is amazing!" Kira said. "I can't believe a place like this is in Iron City!"

"Iron City is not as ugly as you think," Noir said. He looked down at the flowers.

"Tsk," he said, picking a bug from a petal. He showed it to Kira. Then he crushed it between his fingers.

bzzzz

SILICATE FLY...
THEY'RE MURDER
ON THE ROSES.

Noir sighed. "They're back. I just sprayed!"

"This is YOUR garden?" asked Kira.

"Mmmaybe," Noir said.

"You grow roses?" asked Kira.

"What if I do?" Noir said. There was anger in his voice.

"It's just . . . " Kira sat down on a rock. "First, I find out that my idol is now evil. Then, I find out that he spends his time growing roses."

"I never asked to be your idol. And I'm not evil. I'm just old enough to know that things aren't as simple as they seem."

"How can right and wrong be anything but simple?" asked Kira.

"In ten years, you'll see," answered Noir. "Nothing is what it seems—me, you, this city . . . nothing."

Noir fell silent. They both sat for a while, listening to the numbers fall and the silicate flies buzz.

Kira looked at Noir. "You said you'd tell me about the Madrassa Incident."

"I changed my mind. Let's go back," said Noir.

"Hey, that's not fair!" said Kira.

"Life is full of letdowns," said Noir, getting up.

"Och, ye cannae be talking out both sides o' yer mouth, lad," said Seeker.

"What do you mean?" asked Noir.

"Ye say it isn't simple. Then ye say that ye won't explain," said Seeker.

Noir thought for a moment. "You're right," he said finally. "I'll tell you."

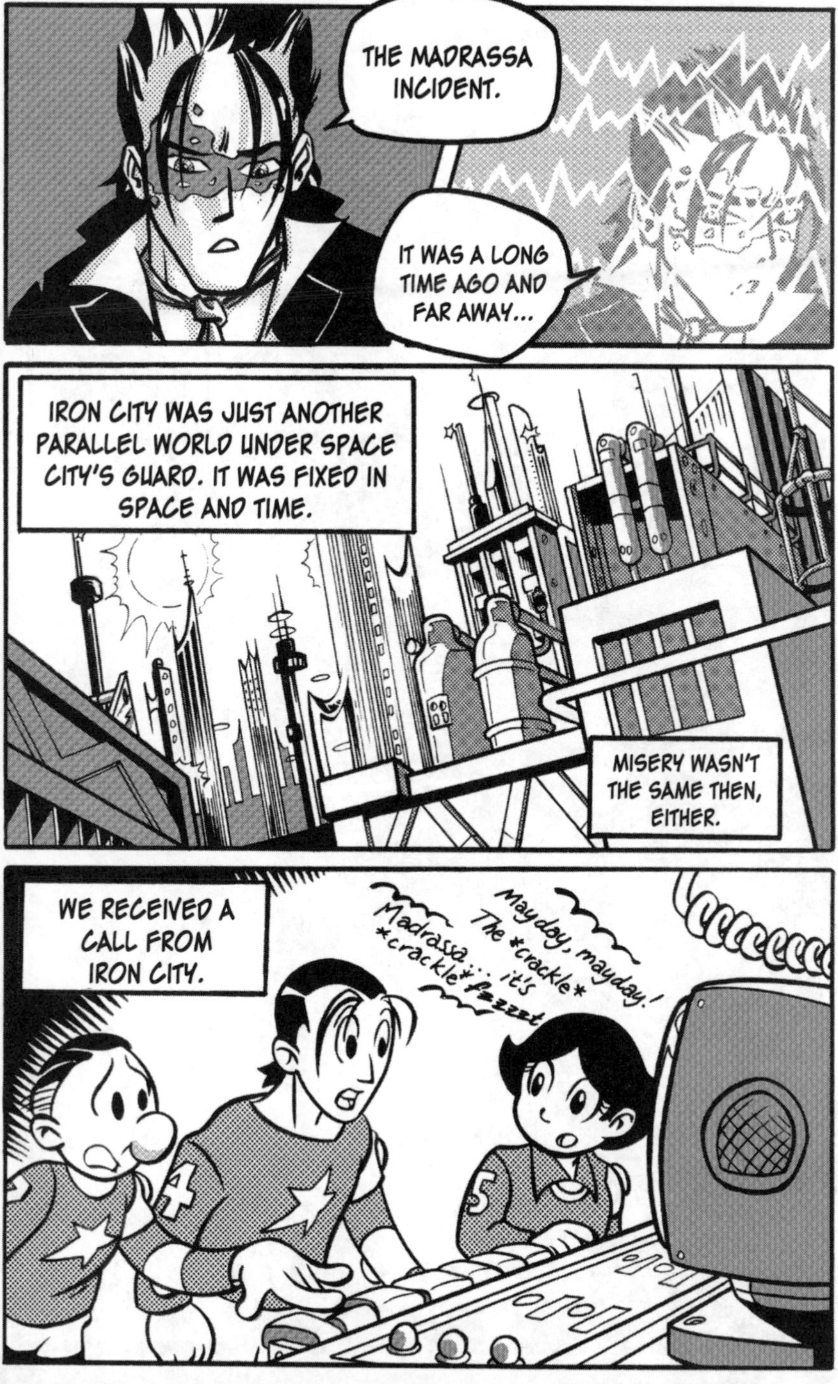
THE MADRASSA INCIDENT.
IT WAS A LONG TIME AGO AND FAR AWAY...
IRON CITY WAS JUST ANOTHER PARALLEL WORLD UNDER SPACE CITY'S GUARD. IT WAS FIXED IN SPACE AND TIME.
MISERY WASN'T THE SAME THEN, EITHER.
WE RECEIVED A CALL FROM IRON CITY.
Mayday, mayday! The *crackle* Madrassa... it's *crackle* fzzzzt

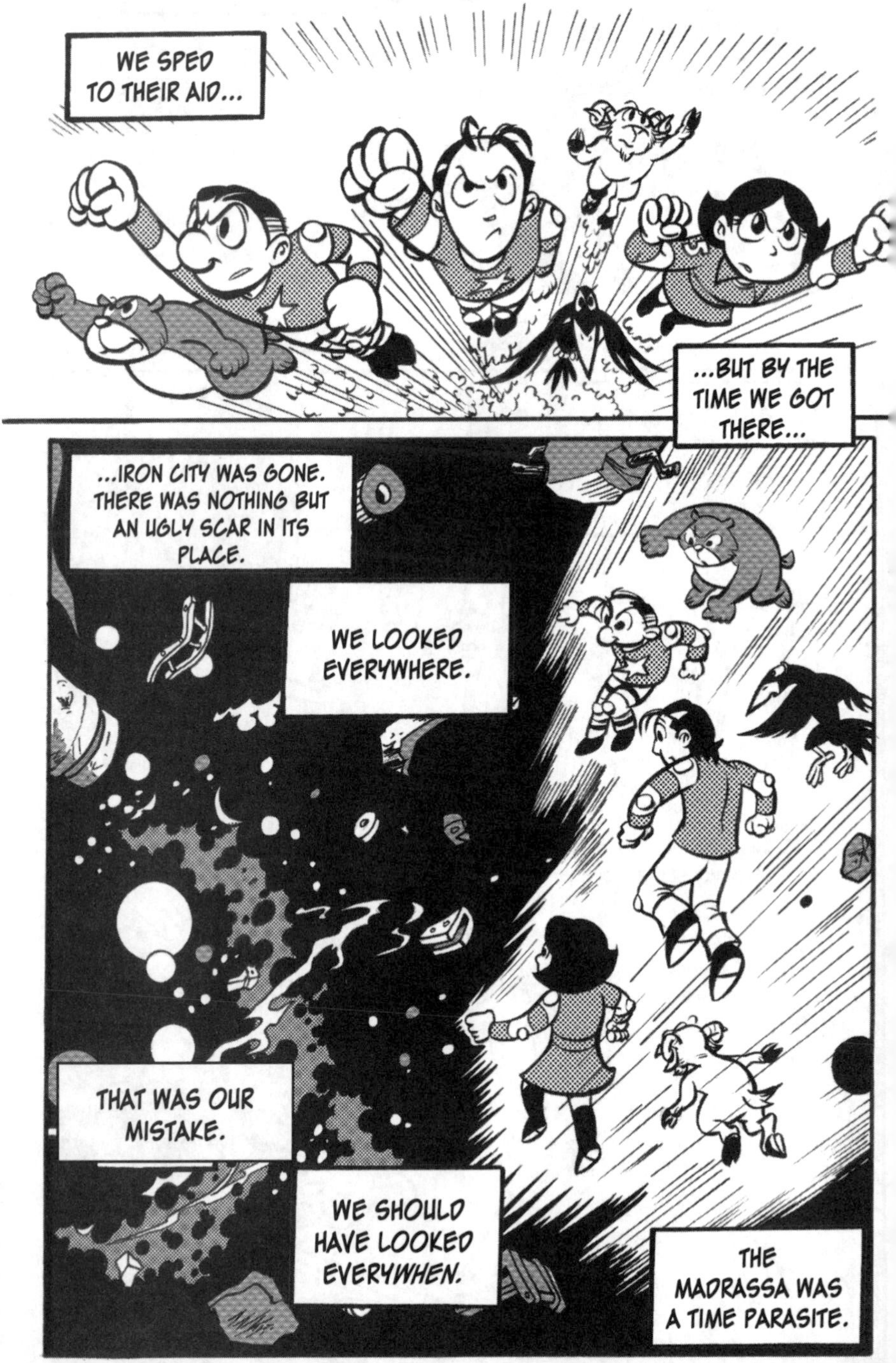
WE SPED TO THEIR AID...
...BUT BY THE TIME WE GOT THERE...
...IRON CITY WAS GONE. THERE WAS NOTHING BUT AN UGLY SCAR IN ITS PLACE.
WE LOOKED EVERYWHERE.
THAT WAS OUR MISTAKE.
WE SHOULD HAVE LOOKED EVERYWHEN.
THE MADRASSA WAS A TIME PARASITE.

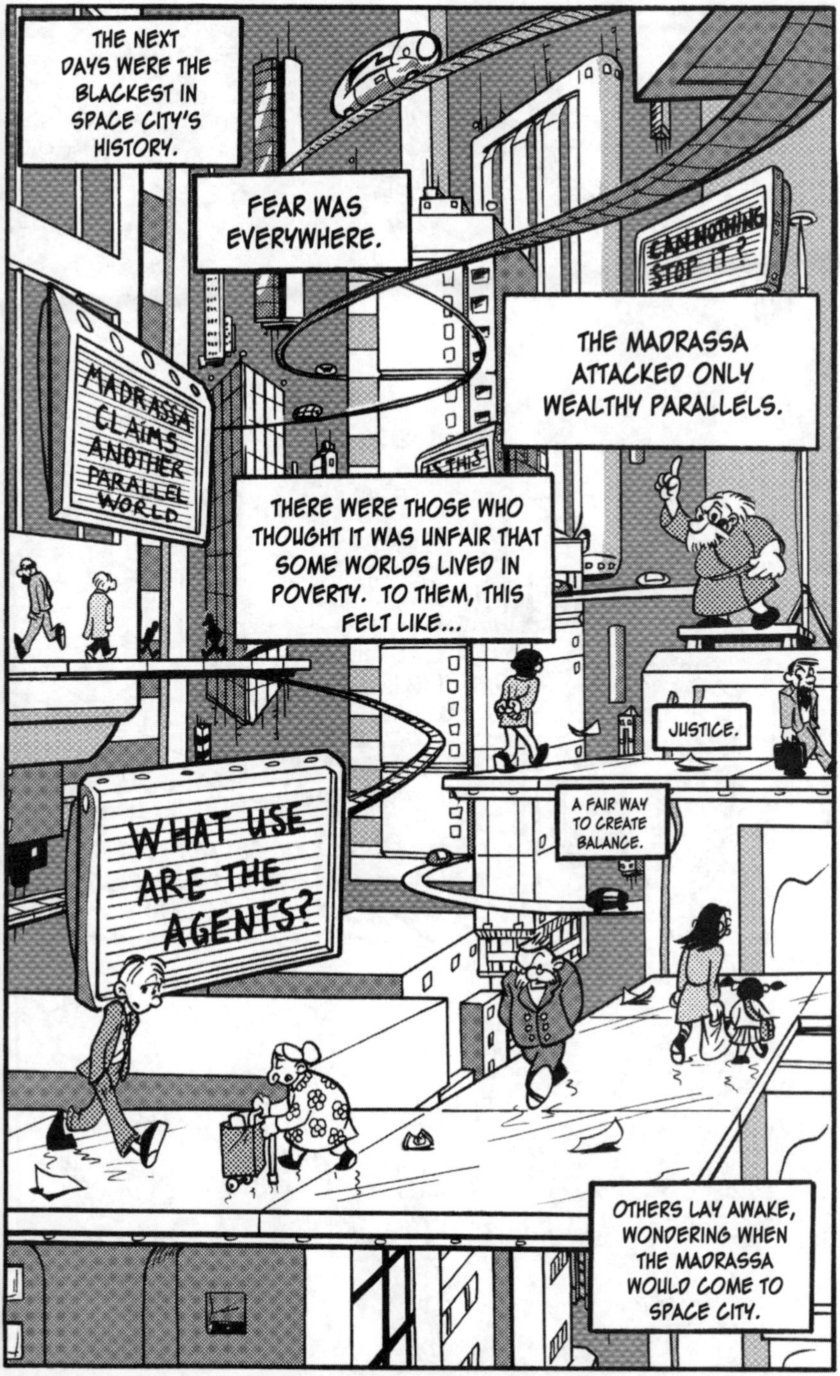
THE NEXT DAYS WERE THE BLACKEST IN SPACE CITY'S HISTORY.
FEAR WAS EVERYWHERE.
CAN NOTHING STOP IT?
THE MADRASSA ATTACKED ONLY WEALTHY PARALLELS.
MADRASSA CLAIMS ANOTHER PARALLEL WORLD
IS THIS
THERE WERE THOSE WHO THOUGHT IT WAS UNFAIR THAT SOME WORLDS LIVED IN POVERTY. TO THEM, THIS FELT LIKE...
JUSTICE.
A FAIR WAY TO CREATE BALANCE.
WHAT USE ARE THE AGENTS?
OTHERS LAY AWAKE, WONDERING WHEN THE MADRASSA WOULD COME TO SPACE CITY.

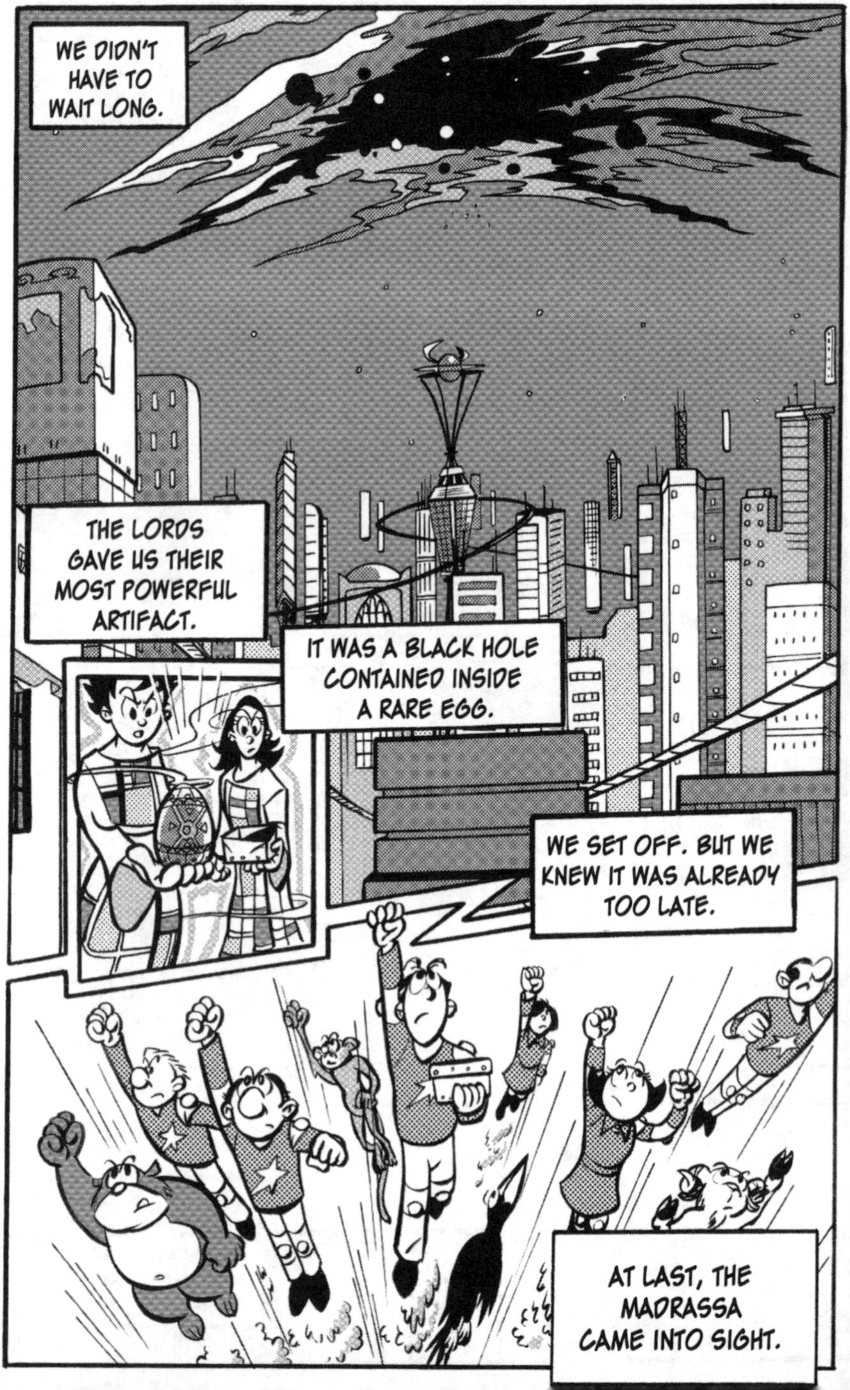
WE DIDN'T HAVE TO WAIT LONG.
THE LORDS GAVE US THEIR MOST POWERFUL ARTIFACT.
IT WAS A BLACK HOLE CONTAINED INSIDE A RARE EGG.
WE SET OFF. BUT WE KNEW IT WAS ALREADY TOO LATE.
AT LAST, THE MADRASSA CAME INTO SIGHT.

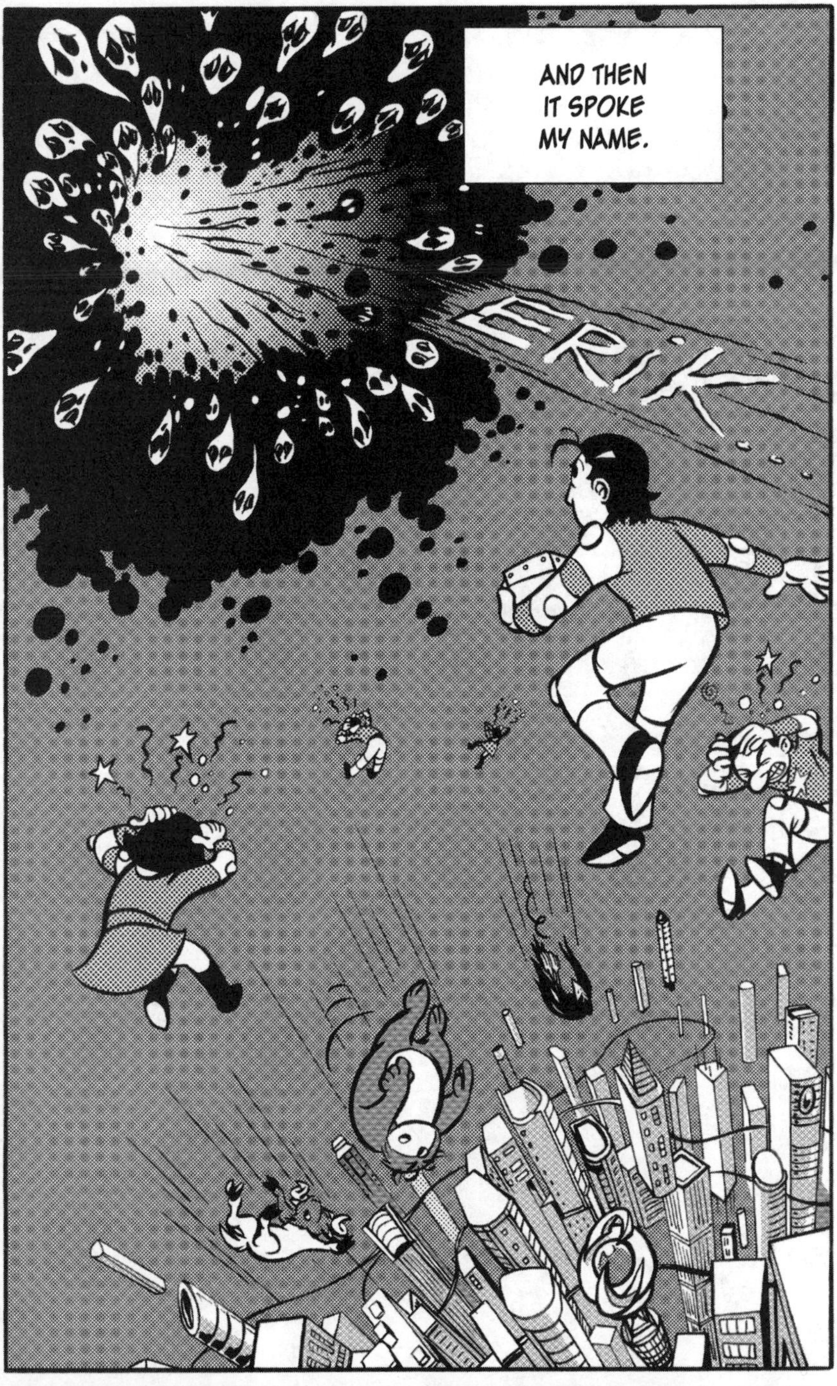
AND THEN IT SPOKE MY NAME.
ERIK...

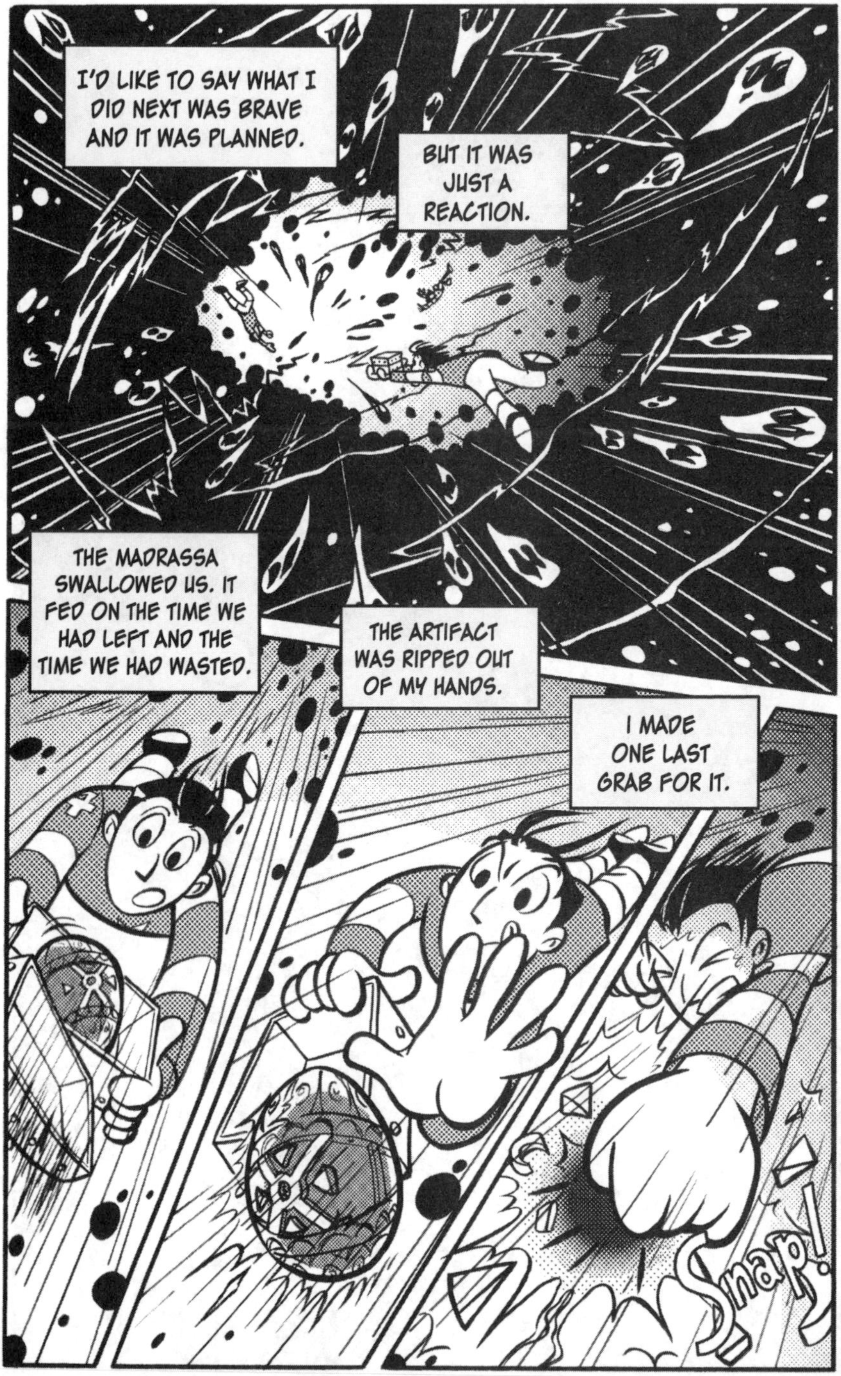
I'D LIKE TO SAY WHAT I DID NEXT WAS BRAVE AND IT WAS PLANNED.
BUT IT WAS JUST A REACTION.
THE MADRASSA SWALLOWED US. IT FED ON THE TIME WE HAD LEFT AND THE TIME WE HAD WASTED.
THE ARTIFACT WAS RIPPED OUT OF MY HANDS.
I MADE ONE LAST GRAB FOR IT.
Snap!

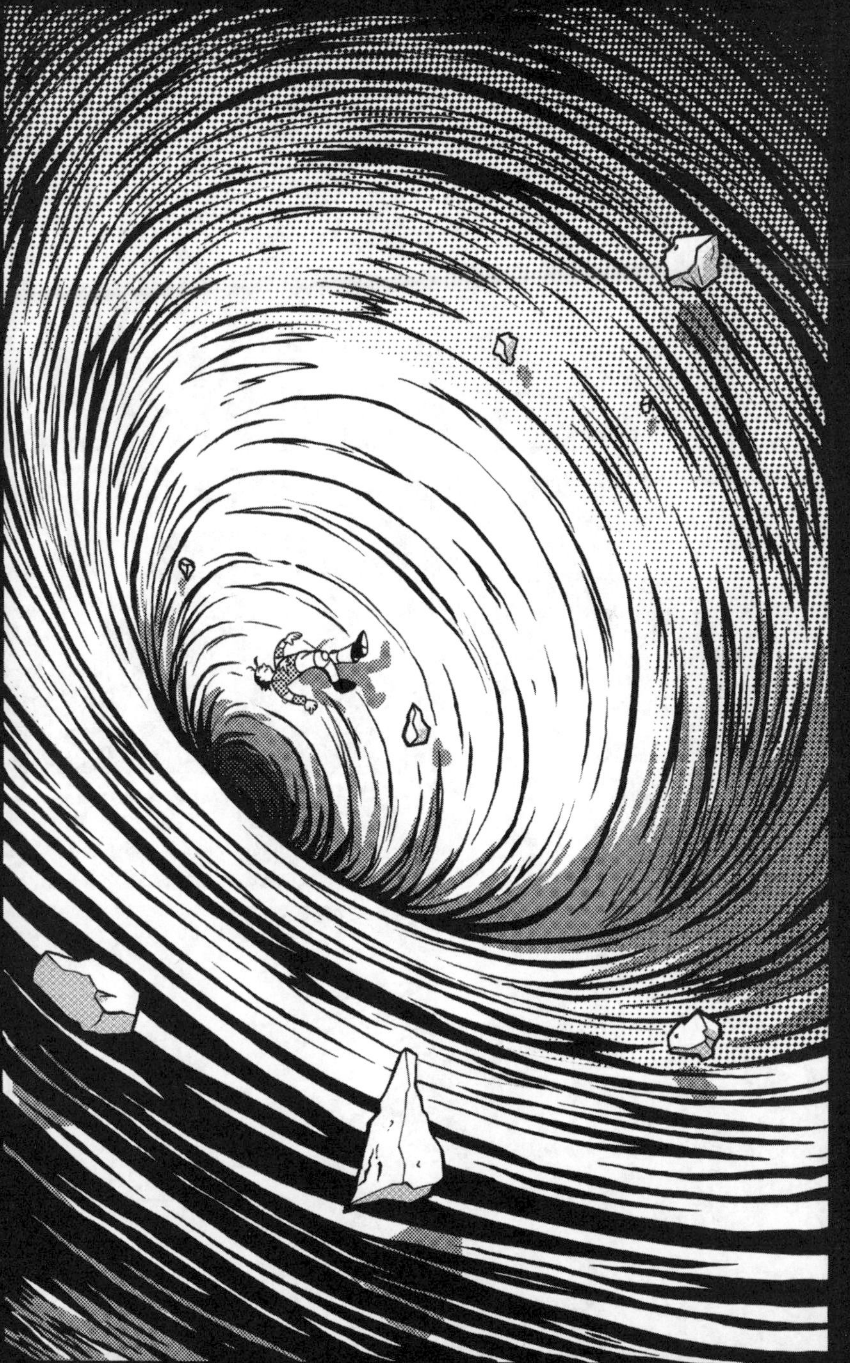

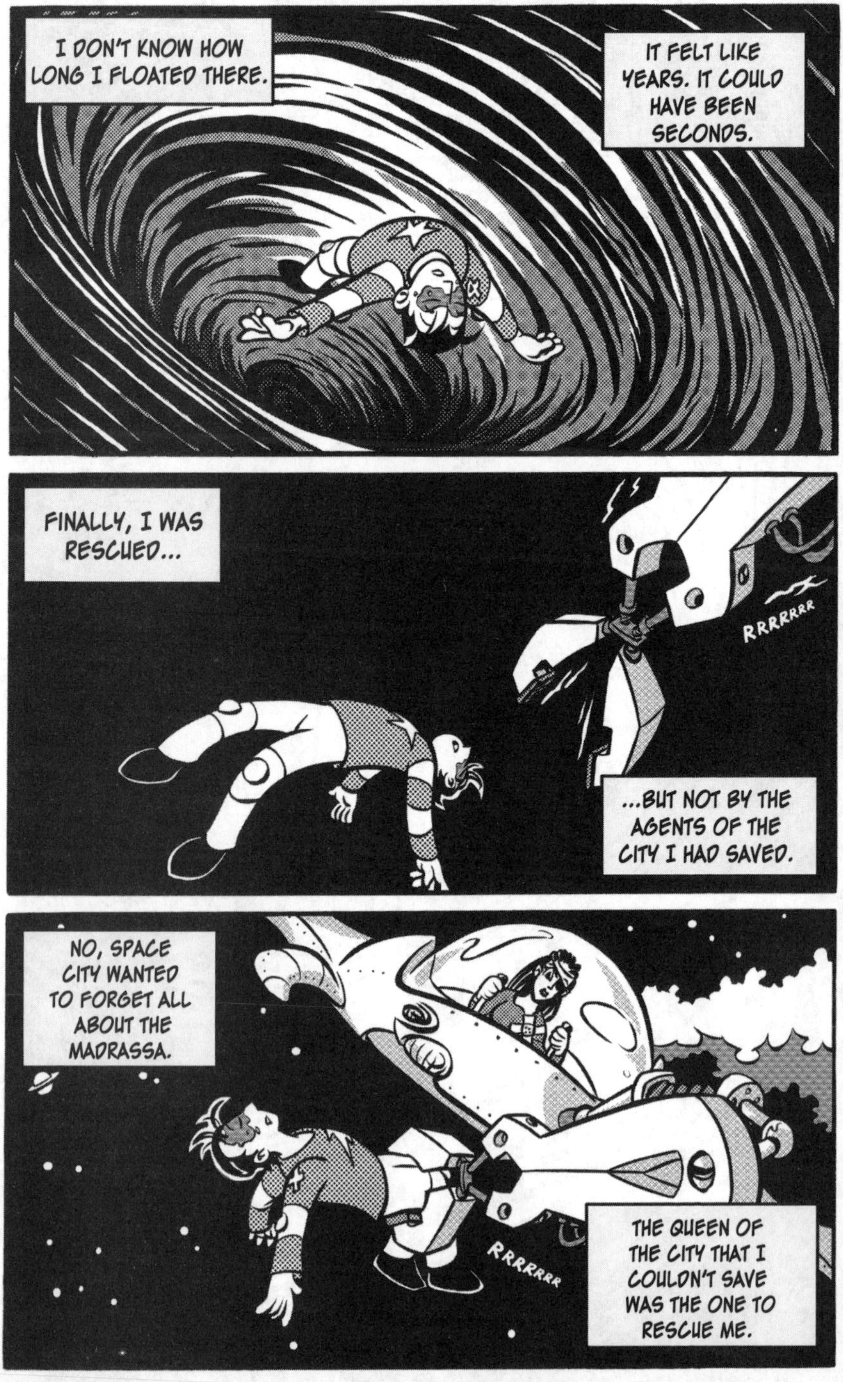
I DON'T KNOW HOW LONG I FLOATED THERE.
IT FELT LIKE YEARS. IT COULD HAVE BEEN SECONDS.
FINALLY, I WAS RESCUED...
RRRRRRR
...BUT NOT BY THE AGENTS OF THE CITY I HAD SAVED.
NO, SPACE CITY WANTED TO FORGET ALL ABOUT THE MADRASSA.
RRRRRRR
THE QUEEN OF THE CITY THAT I COULDN'T SAVE WAS THE ONE TO RESCUE ME.

"Sometimes, people make it through bad things together. Then they don't talk about those times," said Noir. He picked some of the garden's crystal flowers. "But they still share something. Misery saved her city. I saved mine. We share the knowledge of what that cost us."

"That's awful!" cried Kira. "I can't believe the Agents acted that way!"

"Och, I can," said Seeker.

Kira and Noir turned to look at the little badger.

"Ye dinnae get left behind because we wanted to forget the Madrassa," said Seeker. "The Madrassa made us forget. It ate that period of time and our memory of it. Even the Supreme Agent disnae recall what happened. She knows it was very bad, but that's all. We thought ye were dead."

"But . . . " Noir said.

"Nae buts," Seeker said. "Ye have been mad at us all these years. But we dinnae mean to hurt ye. If ye had come back, we could have cleared it up."

Noir stood up. "Yes, well, that is little comfort now. Time to go back to the tower . . . and our front-row seats. The Agents are about to fail Iron City again."

The three made their way back to the Tower. But along the way . . .

"You two go ahead," said Noir. "I have to make a phone call."

Chapter 6
Broken Flowers

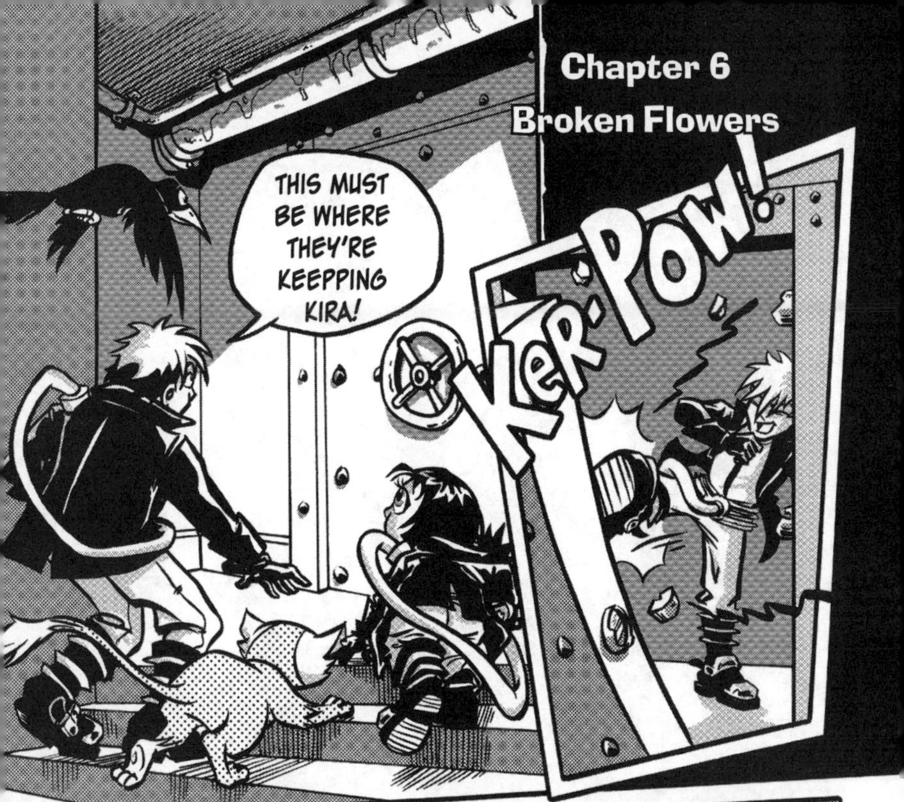
THIS MUST BE WHERE THEY'RE KEEPPING KIRA!
KER-POW!

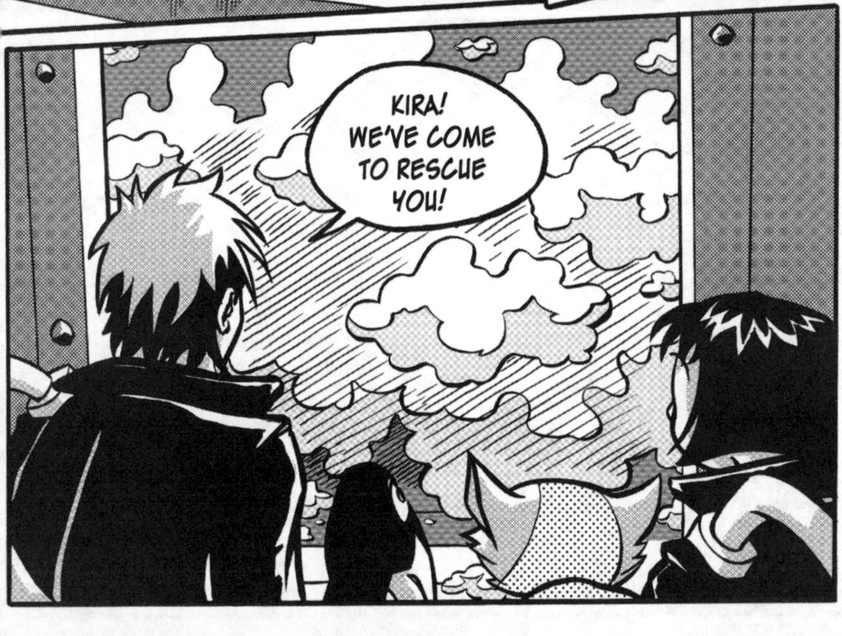
KIRA! WE'VE COME TO RESCUE YOU!

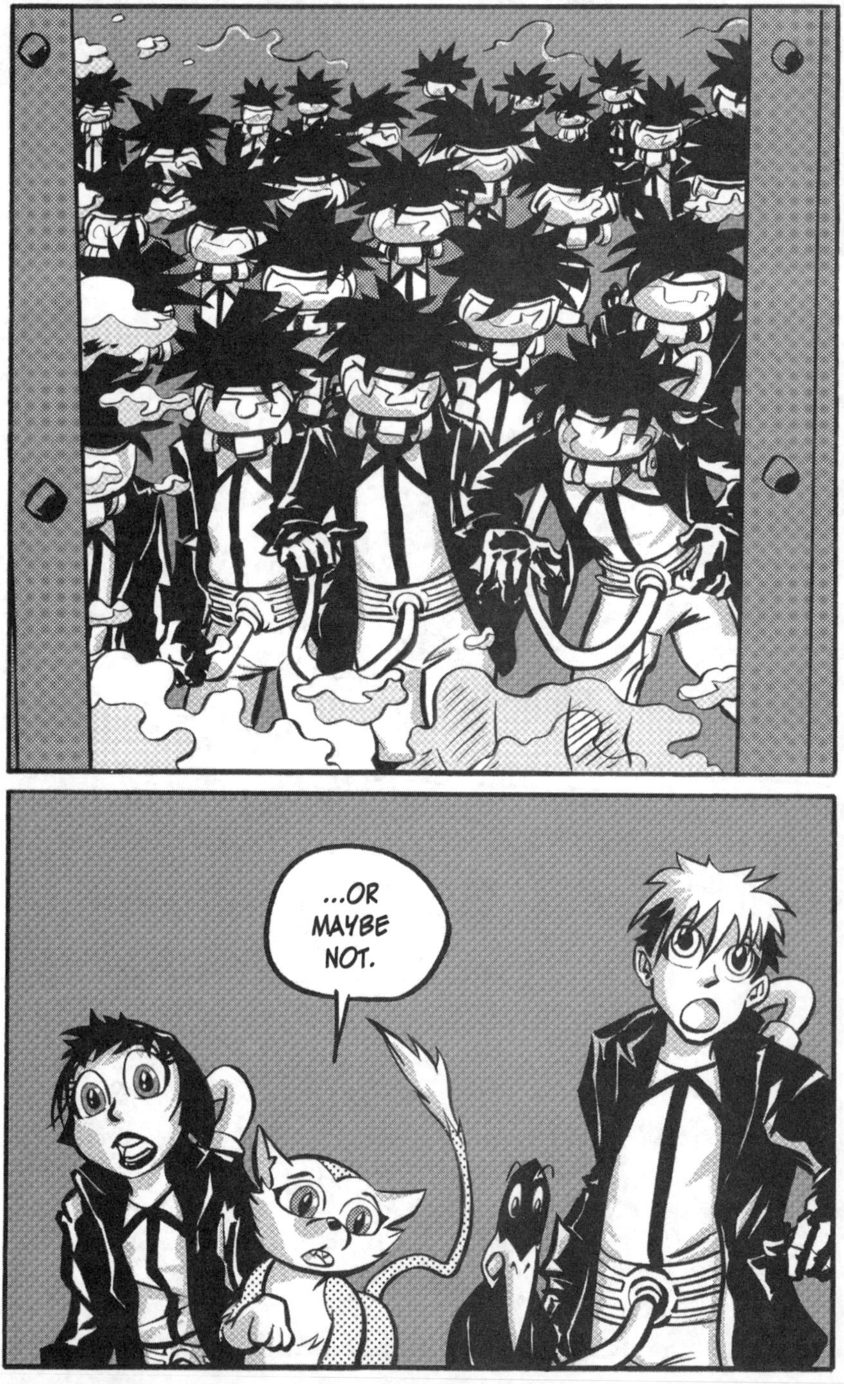
...OR MAYBE NOT.

The kids were taken to the main control room. Boo gasped when she saw the giant Starflower engine in the center of the room!

Queen Misery stood at the controls. There, she kept a beam of energy pointed at the fading sun.

"Sit down," said one of the Commissars. "The Queen will be with you in a moment."

"If Kira wasn't in her room, where is she?" whispered Boo.

At that very moment, three figures came through the door.

"Look!" said Pumpkin. "It's Kira!"

"And Seeker!" added Boo.

AND... *ERIK?!*

Asano jumped to his feet. The person in front of him didn't wear a mask. But it was clearly Noir. And although he had a scar and long hair, it also was clearly his brother Erik.

Noir saw Asano's expression. He raised an eyebrow. "Upset I'm still alive?"

Asano thought back. Erik was so good at everything. Asano had never liked being compared to his brother. But he didn't feel hate. Instead, Asano realized just how much he had missed Erik.

HEY, WATCH THE FLOWERS!

tinkle!

tinkle!

Noir smoothed a few petals in the crushed bouquet of flowers. "You don't know how hard it is to grow these."

"You grow *flowers?*" asked Asano.

"Yeah, want to make something of it?" asked Noir.

"You always were such a GIRL," said Asano.

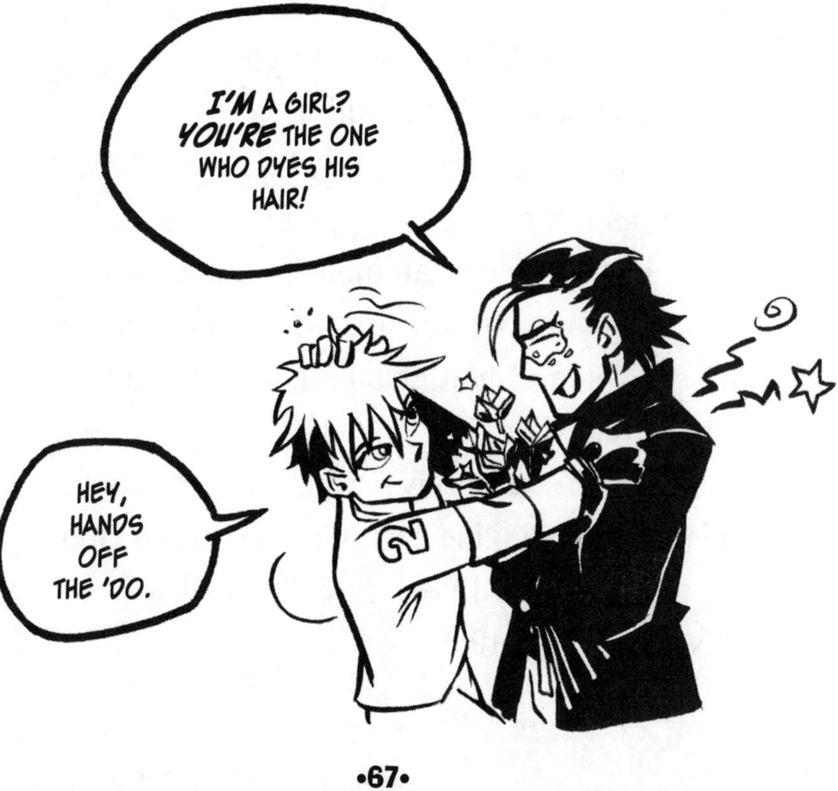
I'M A GIRL? YOU'RE THE ONE WHO DYES HIS HAIR!
HEY, HANDS OFF THE 'DO.

Iron City's star shook. Then the entire city shook!

Misery looked up from her work. "Less hugging, people!" she shouted. "Some of us need to focus!"

Kira joined Asano and Boo.

Noir stood next to his queen. He lay down the flowers. "These are for you," he said. "I know you don't have time for them now. But I still wanted to give them to you."

"Thank you," she said.

"Um, excuse me," cut in Pumpkin. "Want to let us in on what's happening here?"

"If you keep talking, we have a very small chance of survival. Shut up and let me focus, and that chance is a little better," answered Misery.

"But if we survive, what happens to the places you're taking energy from?" asked Boo.

"Do I look like I care?" asked Misery. "Now SHUT UP."

"Erik . . . " Asano said. Noir just shook his head.

Boo felt something in her pocket. It was the Artifact. The lump was moving. And it had become brighter!

"Throw it in the engine!" said Asano.

"No," said Boo. "I'm SURE that's not what it's for. Throw something ELSE in the engine!"

"Hmm . . . " said Asano. "Do me a favor?"

"Mmmaybe," said Boo. Doing favors for Asano often meant getting in trouble. "What do I have to do?"

JUST GO TALK TO OUR NICE FRIEND MISERY OVER THERE.

BUT...SHE'S NOT NICE AT ALL!

"Do I have to?" asked Boo.

"YES!" said Asano and Kira. They had come up with a plan.

"NO!" said Boo. "Not until you tell me what's going on."

"Remember when Asano made up slamball moves and I threw a tantrum?"

"Yeah," said Boo.

"We're going to do something like that."

"I can't handle Queen Misery AND a Kira-tantrum," said Boo.

"I won't have a tantrum!" yelled Kira. "Now go talk to Queen Misery!"

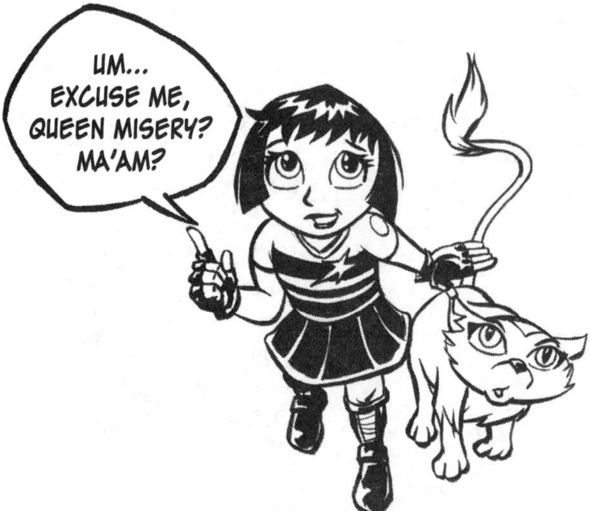
UM...
EXCUSE ME,
QUEEN MISERY?
MA'AM?

"What?" asked Misery.

"Would you like to go back to Space City for some tea?" said Boo. "Instead of getting blown up?"

"No," said Misery.

"It's very good tea," said Boo. "And we have chocolate cookies."

Queen Misery looked up. "Has it never crossed your little pea brain that I don't want to leave my home? Or that I don't care what happens to the Multiverse? It's never done a thing to help me."

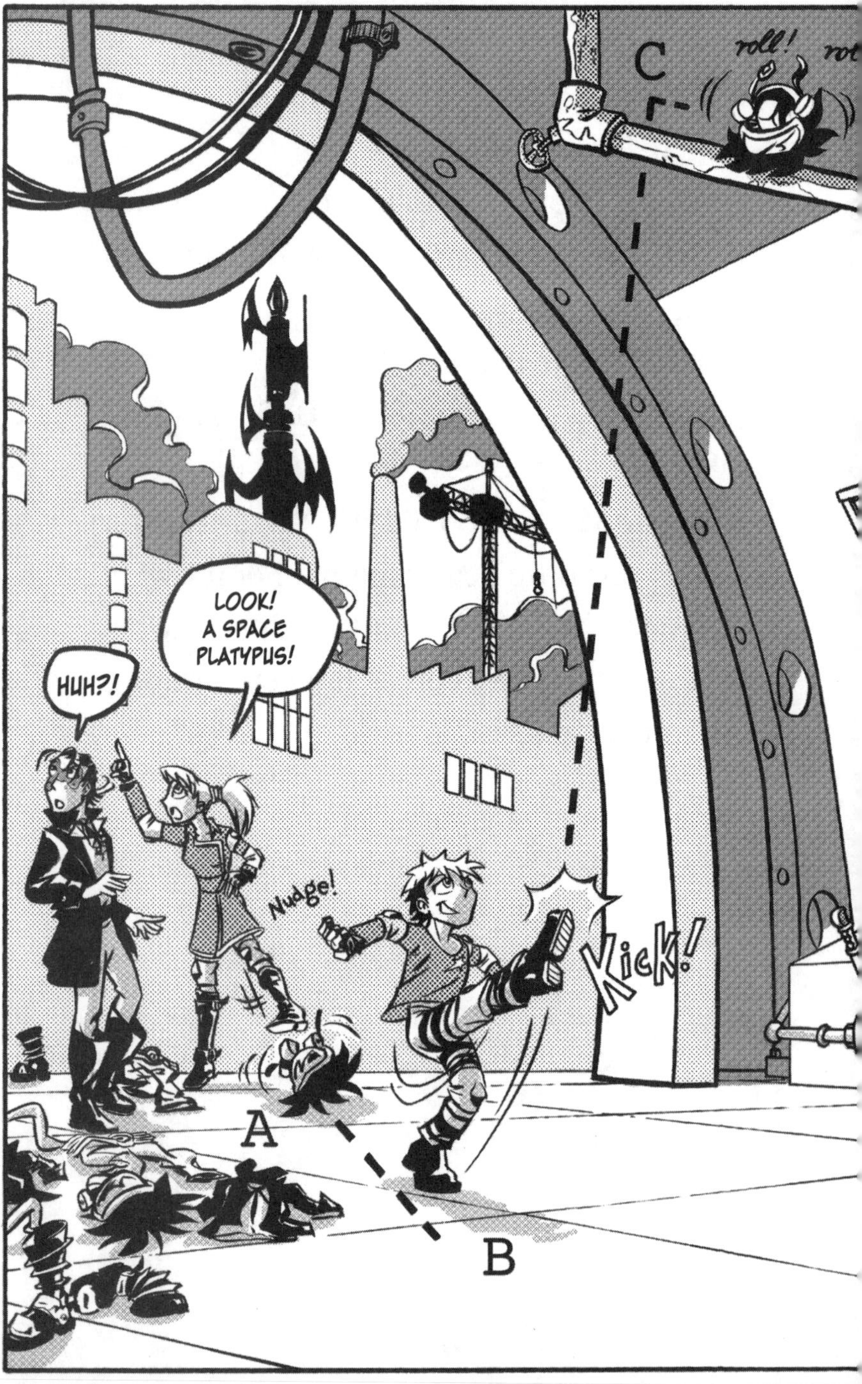
C
roll!
LOOK!
A SPACE
PLATYPUS!
HUH?!
Nudge!
KICK!
A
B

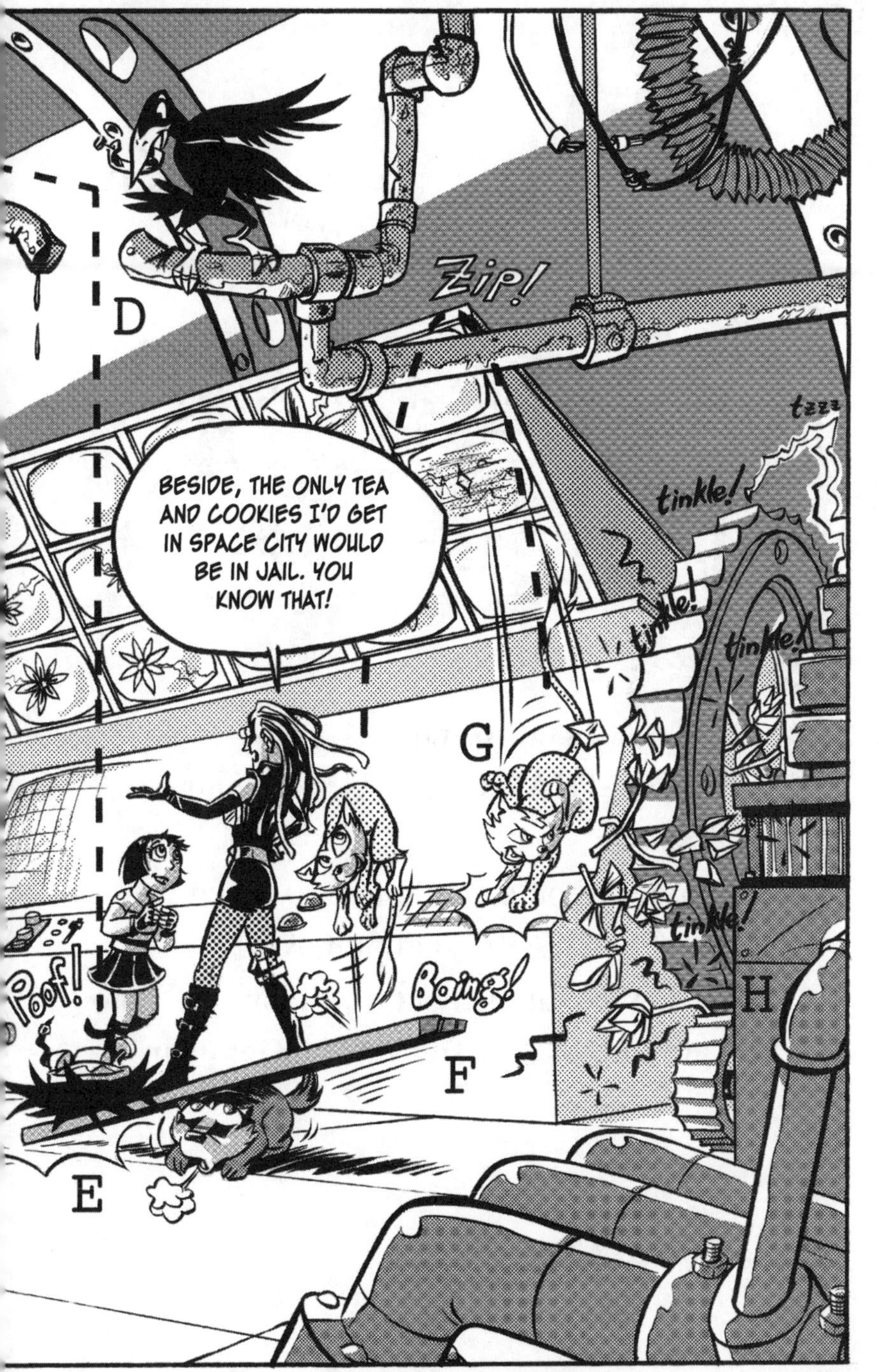

BESIDE, THE ONLY TEA AND COOKIES I'D GET IN SPACE CITY WOULD BE IN JAIL. YOU KNOW THAT!
Zip!
tzzz
tinkle!
tinkle!
tinkle!
tinkle!
D
G
Poof!
Boing!
F
H
E

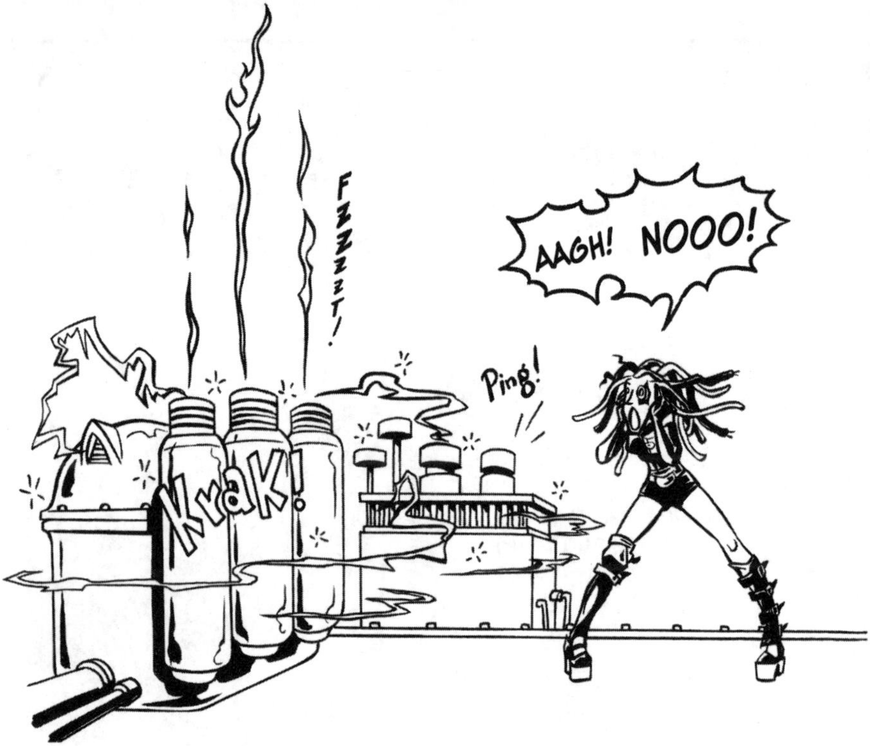
FZZZZZT!
AAGH! NOOO!
Ping!
KraK!

"Cool!" said Asano.

"Now THAT's what I call teamwork," said Kira.

"What should we do now?" asked Boo.

"RUN AWAY!" said Pumpkin.

The kids jumped out a window and onto the ground. Misery screamed, "Get them!"

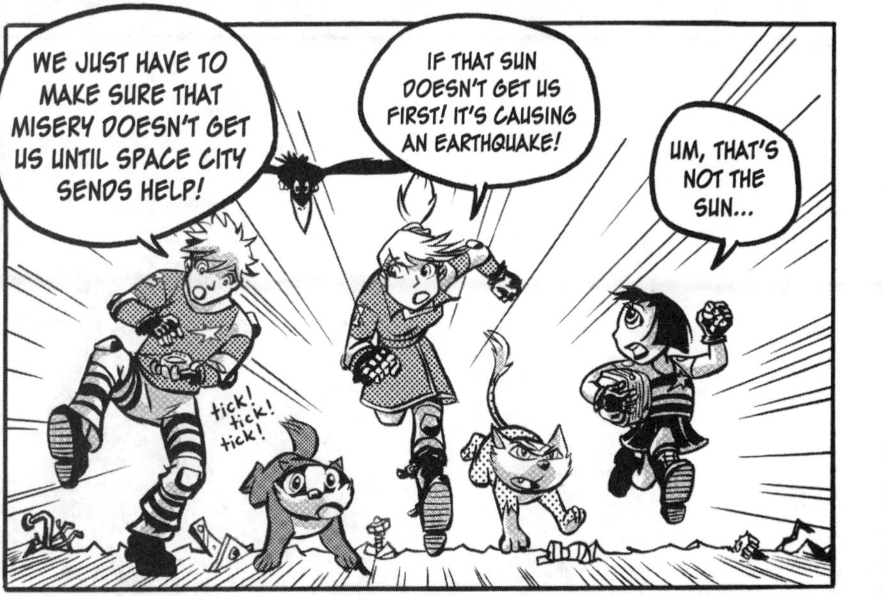
WE JUST HAVE TO MAKE SURE THAT MISERY DOESN'T GET US UNTIL SPACE CITY SENDS HELP!
IF THAT SUN DOESN'T GET US FIRST! IT'S CAUSING AN EARTHQUAKE!
UM, THAT'S NOT THE SUN...
tick! tick! tick!

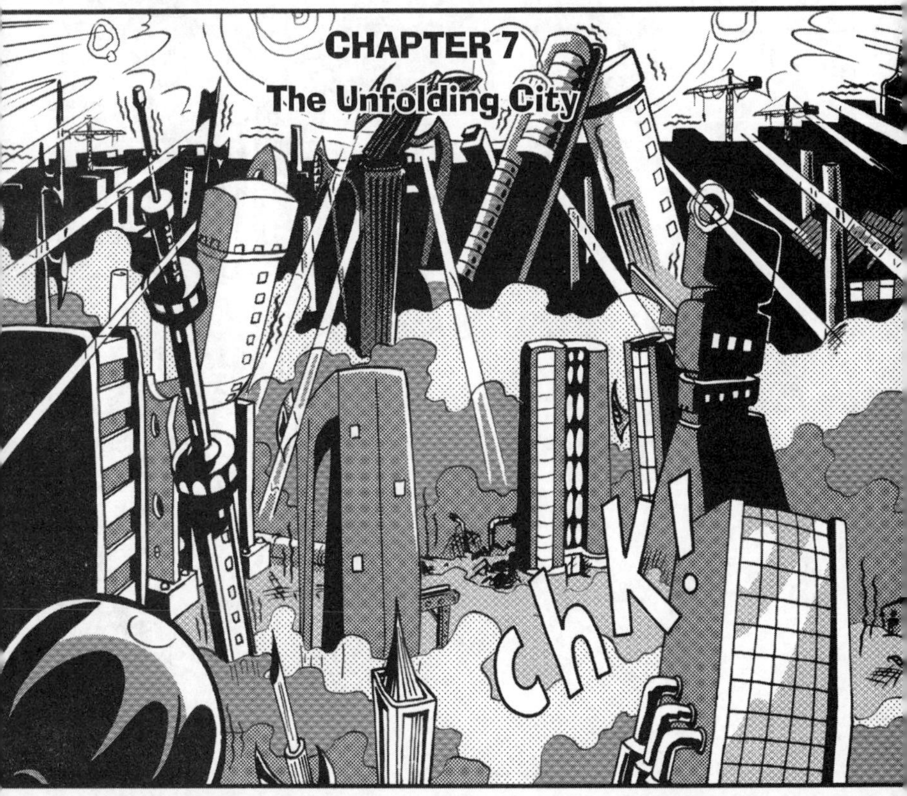
CHAPTER 7
The Unfolding City
ChK!

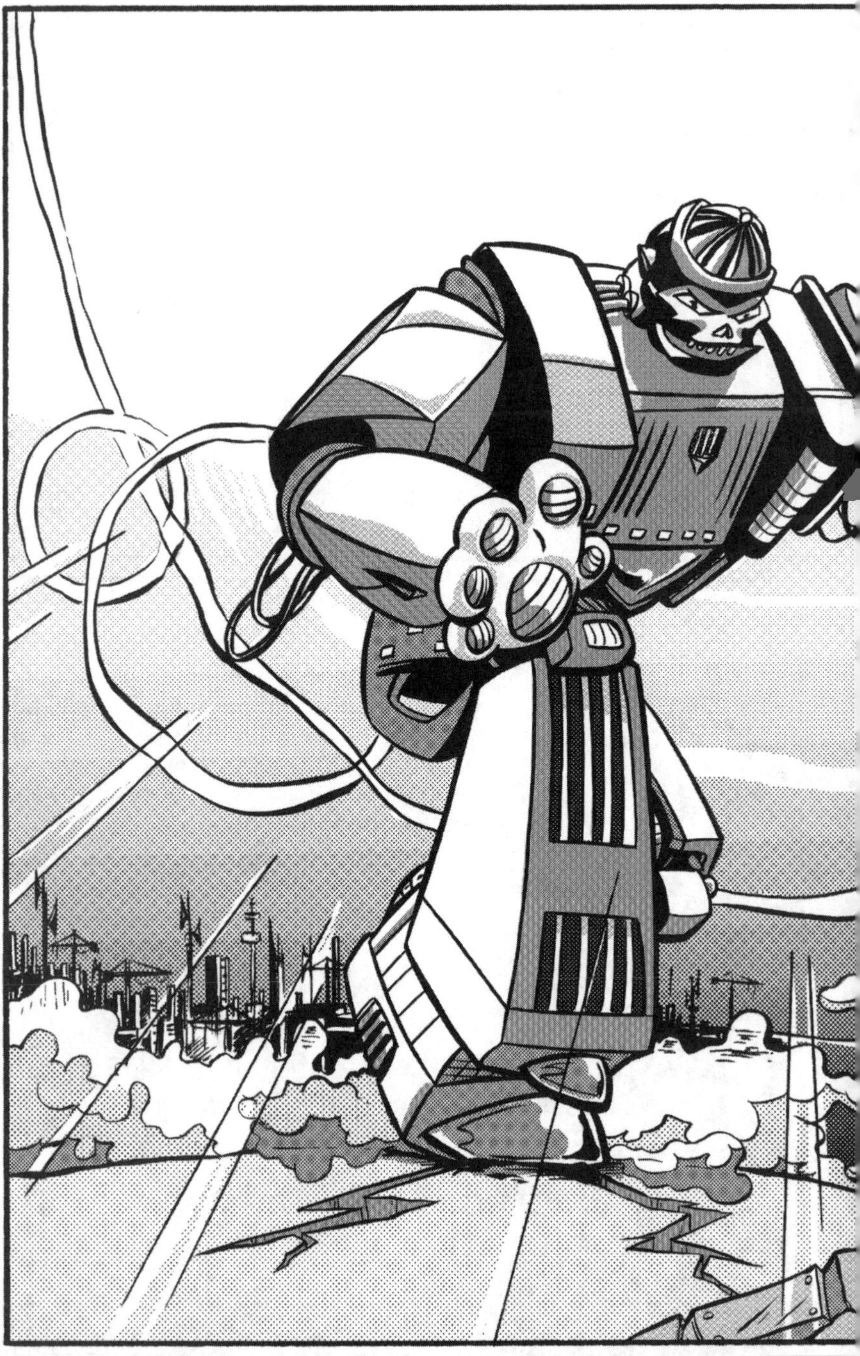

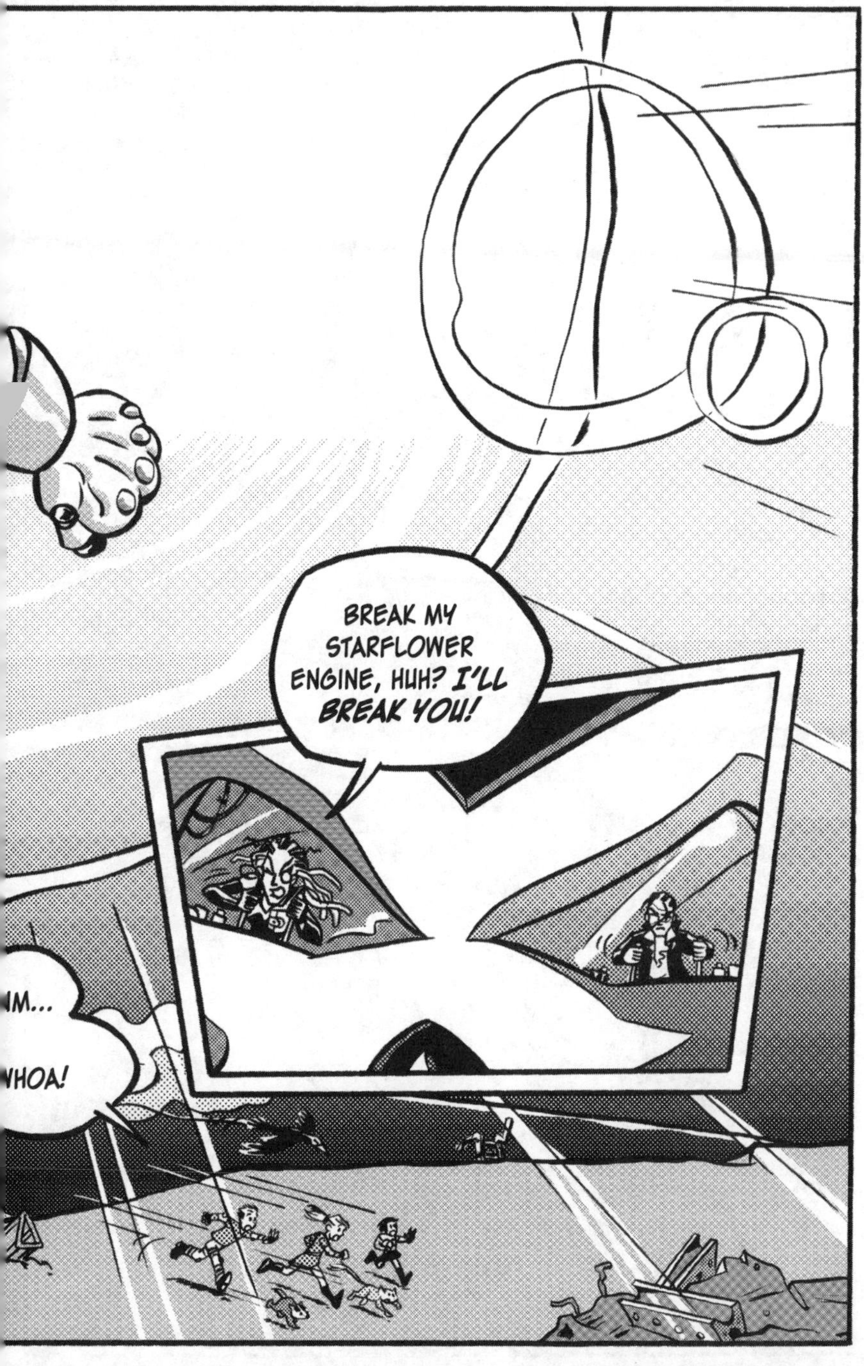
BREAK MY STARFLOWER ENGINE, HUH? I'LL BREAK YOU!
...M...
...WHOA!

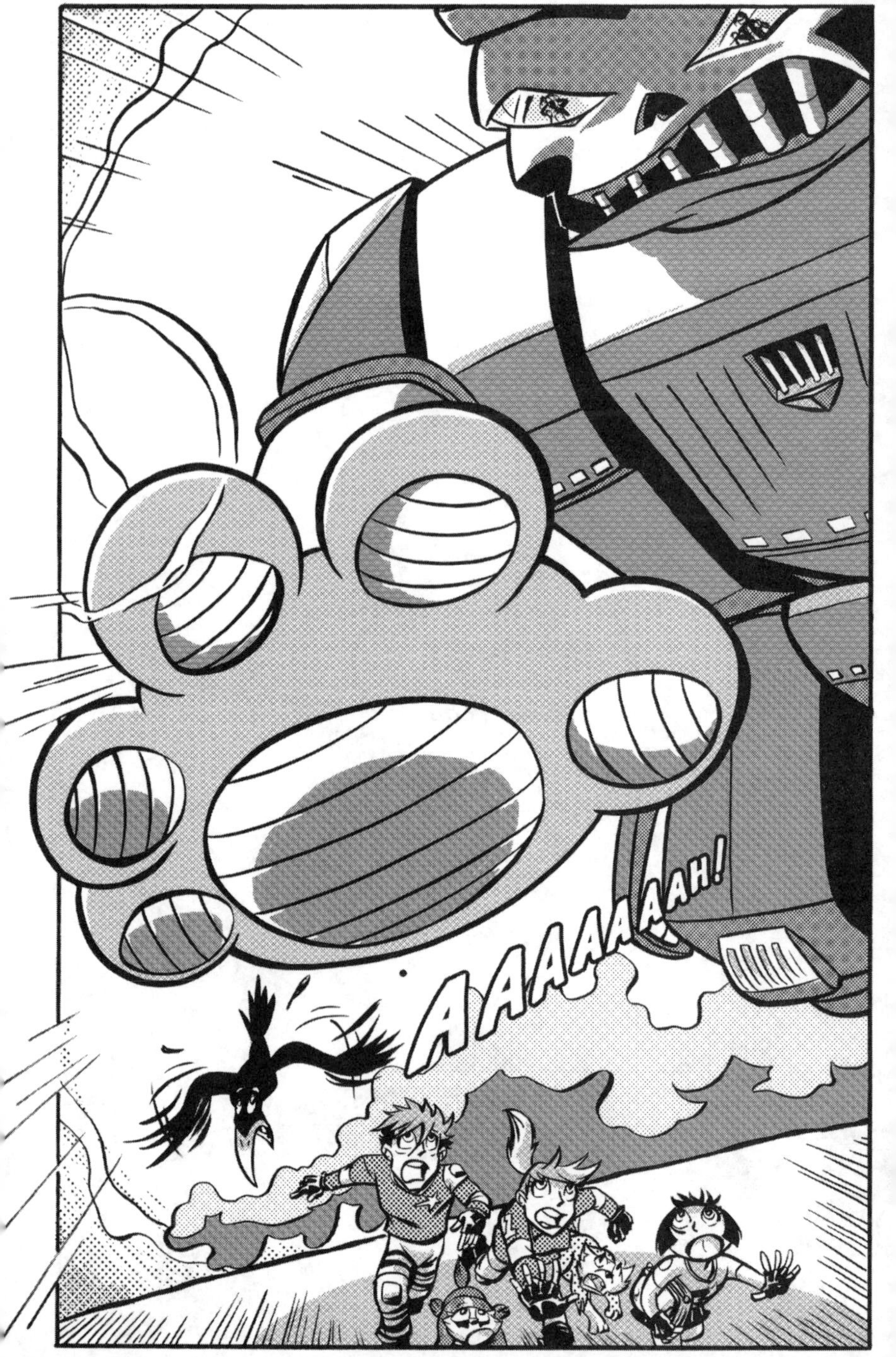
AAAAAAAAH!

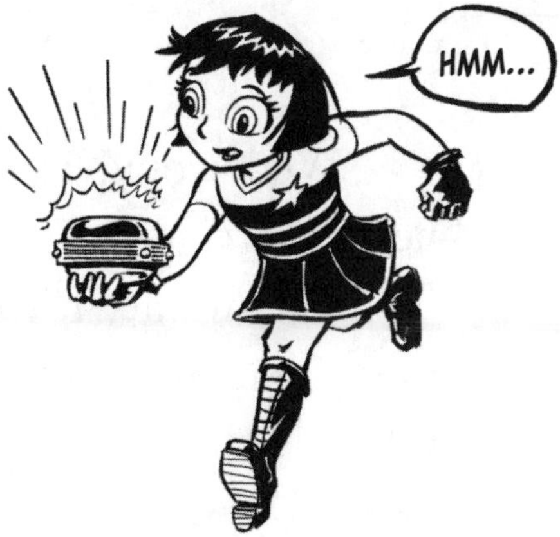
HMM...

They ran for their lives.

"What do we do, oh great and wise team leader?" Asano asked Kira.

"I don't know!" cried Kira. "I skipped the 'what to do when chased by a giant robot' lesson!"

"We could ditch these Iron City losers and head home," said Pumpkin.

"I don't want to leave my brother," said Asano. "It was bad enough losing him once."

"And I want to show Misery and Noir that people do help," said Kira. "If we could just find a place to move Iron City . . ."

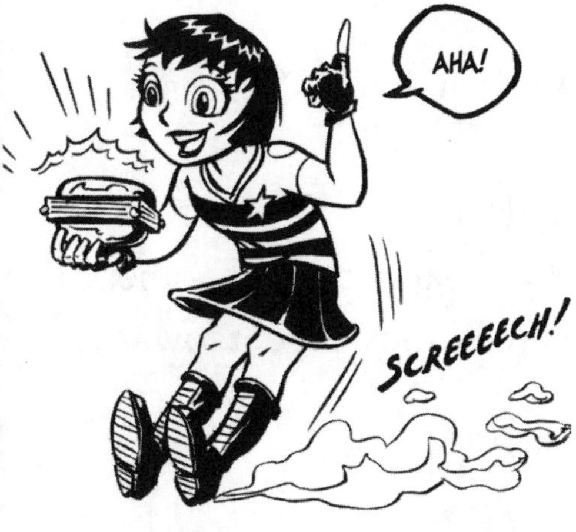
AHA!
SCREEEECH!

"Who would want the Commissars as neighbors?" asked Asano.

"Follow me, I'll explain on the way!" said Boo. She ran back toward the giant robot.

BOO, WHAT ARE YOU DOING?

"Kid, are you CRAZY?" asked Pumpkin.

"Trust me," said Boo.

Kira and Asano looked at each other. Then they followed the littlest Agent toward the robot.

Boo was sure what she was doing was right. But she felt scared and wanted to run. The giant robot closed its cold iron fist around them. It raised them up and up.

Soon, they were hundreds of feet above the ground. Then they saw Queen Misery.

"W-what does that mean?" asked Kira.

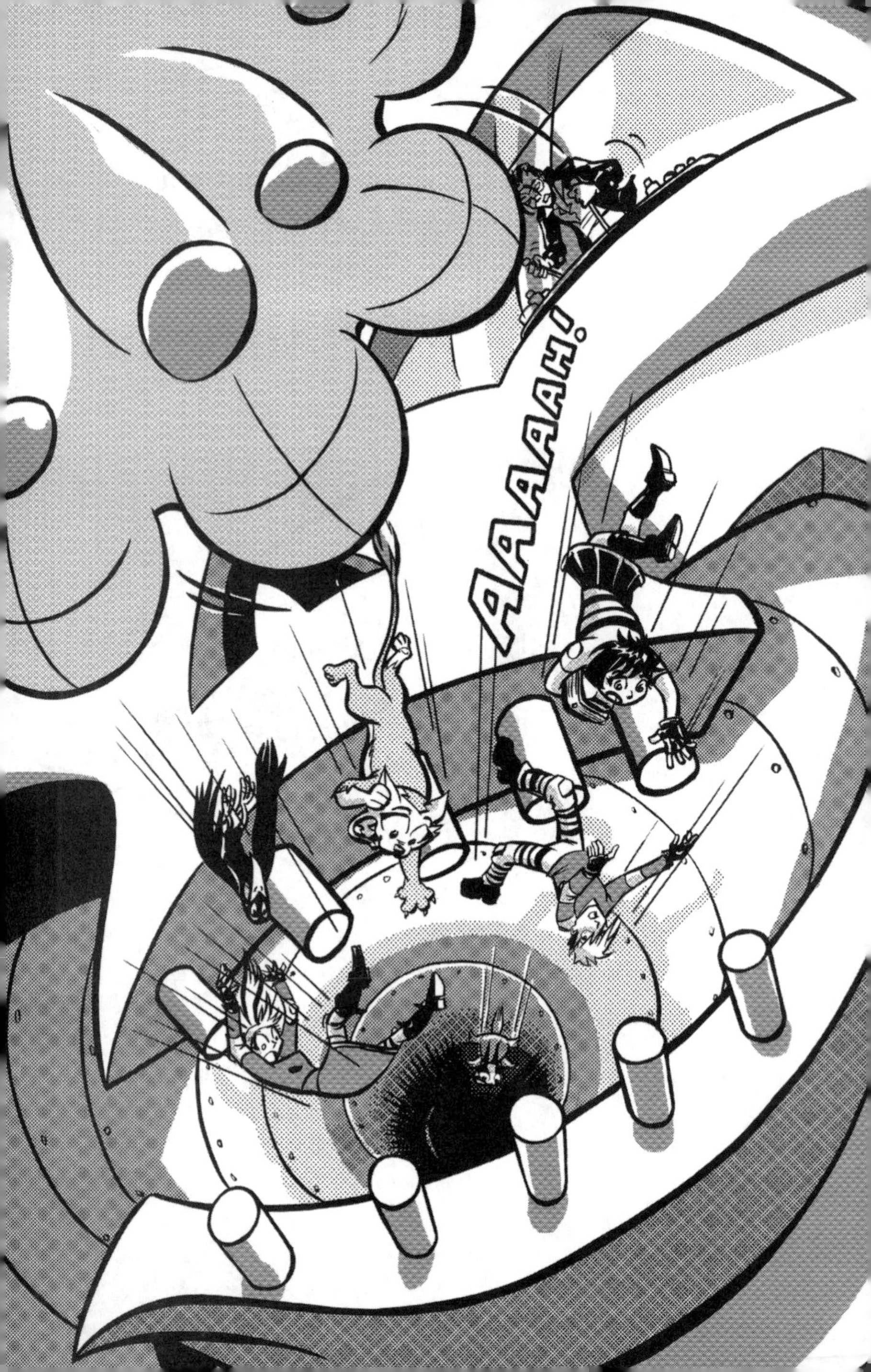
AAAAAH!

Chapter 8:
The Heart of Gold

The robot's mouth was like a large metal cave. Giant metal teeth blocked its only exit. Outside, Iron City's sun had swollen to fill the whole sky. Even the little light that made it through the big teeth was blinding.

"Is everyone okay?" asked Kira.

"Yes, fine!" said Boo. "The floor is softer than I thought it would be!"

"That's because you didn't land on the floor," said Pumpkin. "You landed on me!"

"Oh! I'm so sorry!" said Boo.

"That's okay," said Pumpkin. "All in the line of duty."

"But why, Agent Boo, did you run back toward the robot-city? Now we're held by an enemy without pity," said Quoth.

"Because the Lords said—" began Boo. But she didn't finish. A door at the back of the robot's mouth had opened. Noir and Queen Misery entered. Misery frowned at the kids. Her glass eye flashed in the bright light.

"Are ye g-g-going to kill us?" asked a scared Seeker. Giant robots, metal spiders, and a swelling sun were too much for the poor badger.

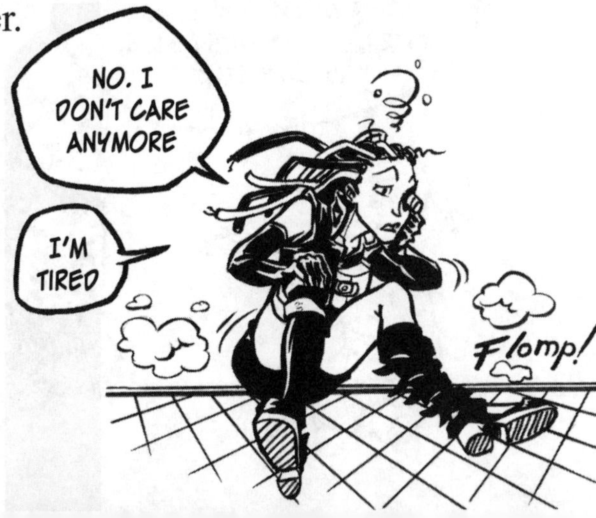
NO. I DON'T CARE ANYMORE
I'M TIRED
Flomp!

The kids just stared.

"I just don't have the energy," Misery sighed. "All the hate . . . it's never brought me anything but . . . misery."

The sun sparked and sputtered in the sky. Boo felt the metal robot growing warm.

The flash caught Misery's eye. "We're all about to die anyway. I traded something precious so Iron City could hop through Parallels. But running away didn't save us . . . it just delayed the end."

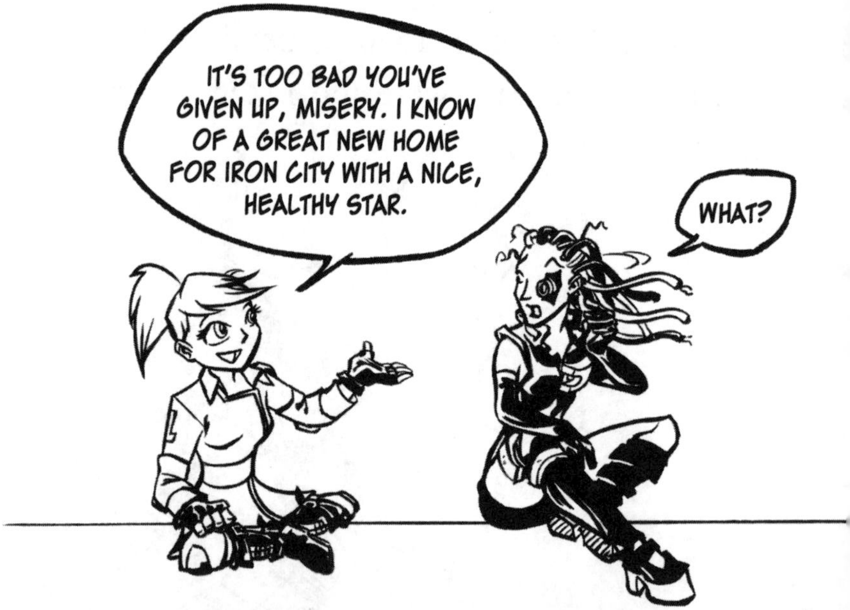
IT'S TOO BAD YOU'VE GIVEN UP, MISERY. I KNOW OF A GREAT NEW HOME FOR IRON CITY WITH A NICE, HEALTHY STAR.
WHAT?

"It would be a lot of work getting used to a new place," said Kira. "But if Iron City can make one last hop, it could find a home for good."

Misery cried out. "But I've been so nasty to all of you! Why do you want to help me? Is this a trick?"

"We think you've punished yourself enough already," said Kira. "And much better than we ever could."

"Yep!" added Boo.

"How do we know we can trust you?" asked Noir.

BECAUSE WE WANT TO GIVE YOU THIS!

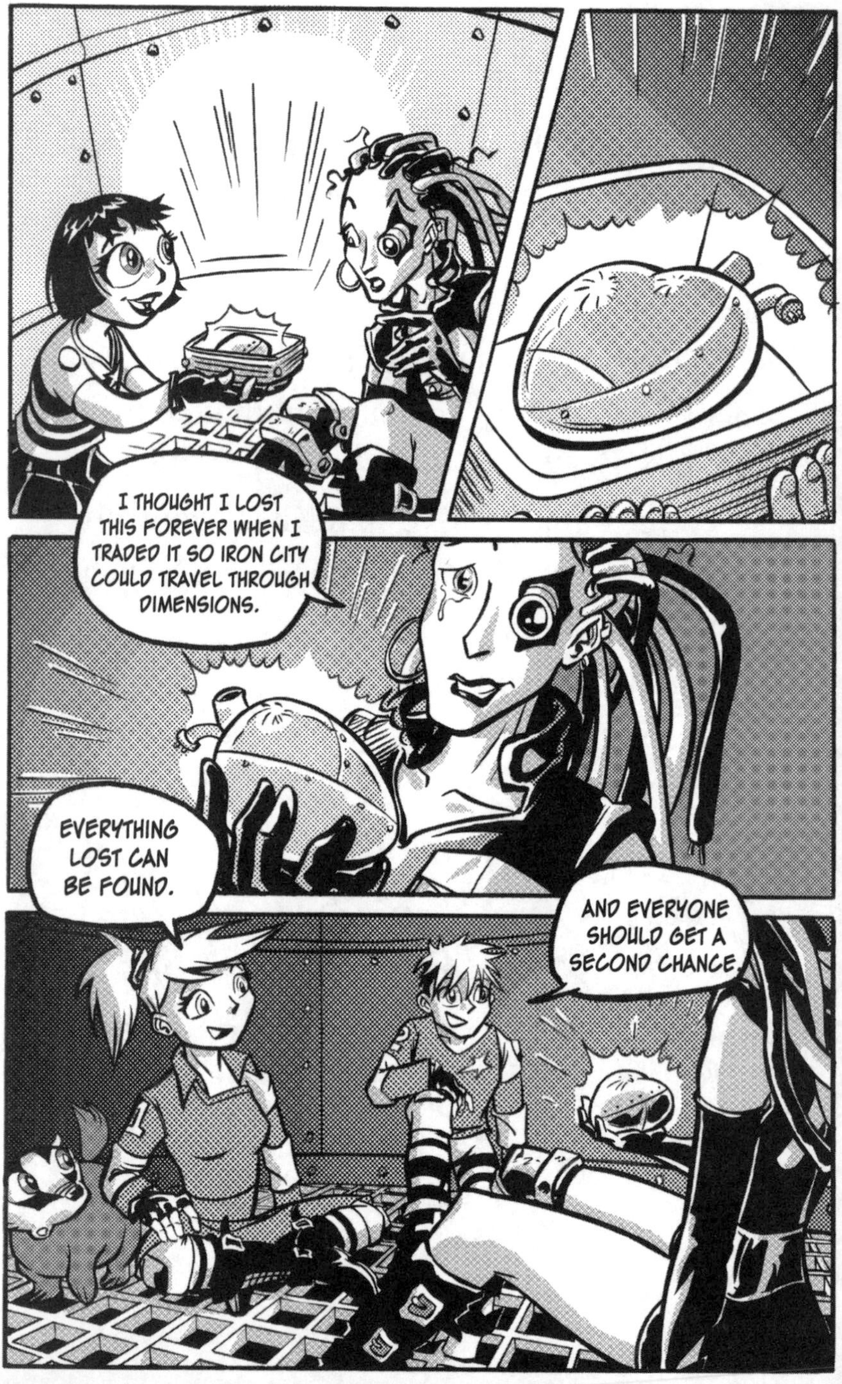
I THOUGHT I LOST THIS FOREVER WHEN I TRADED IT SO IRON CITY COULD TRAVEL THROUGH DIMENSIONS.
EVERYTHING LOST CAN BE FOUND.
AND EVERYONE SHOULD GET A SECOND CHANCE.

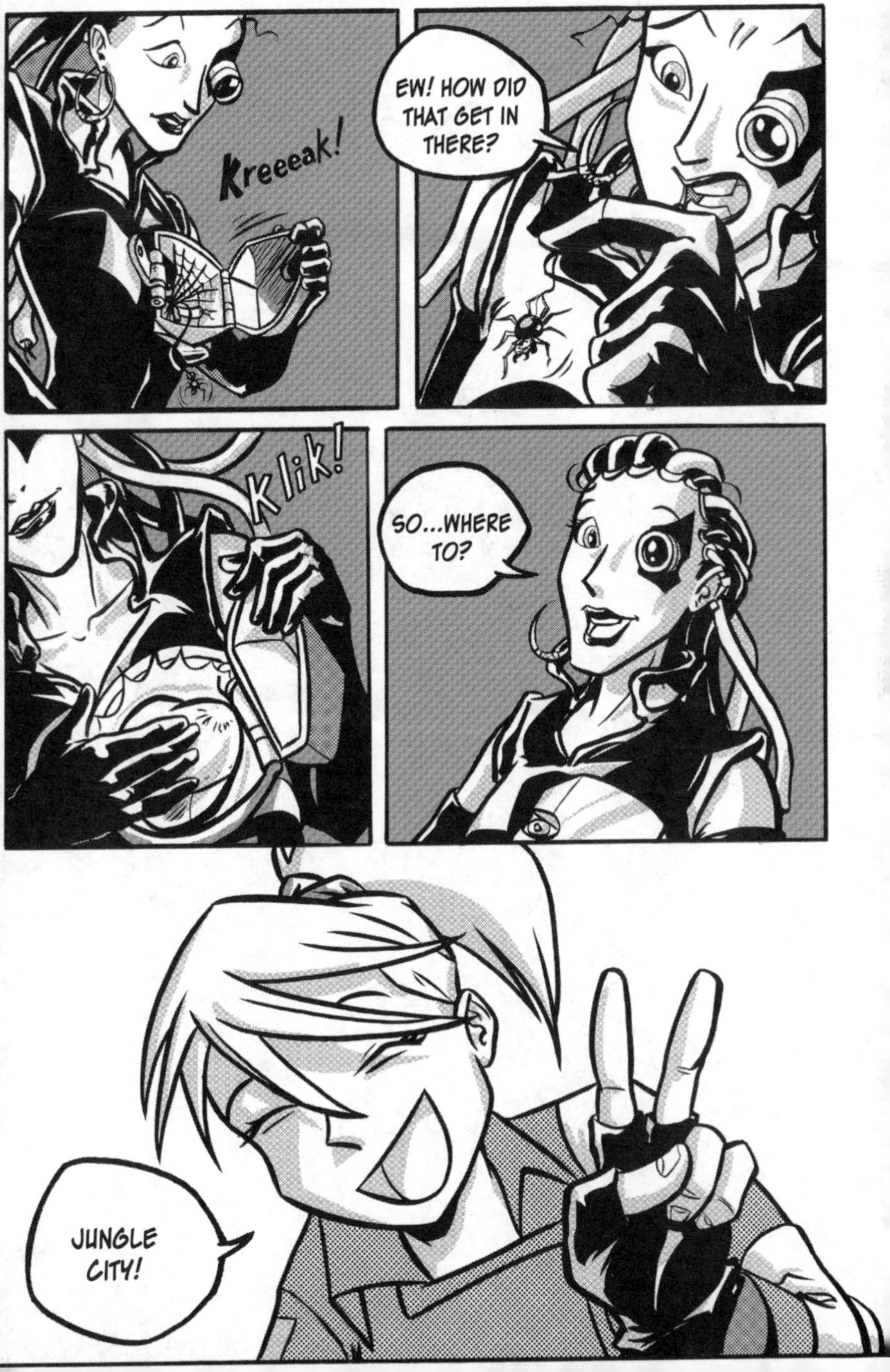
Kreeeak!
EW! HOW DID THAT GET IN THERE?
Klik!
SO...WHERE TO?
JUNGLE CITY!

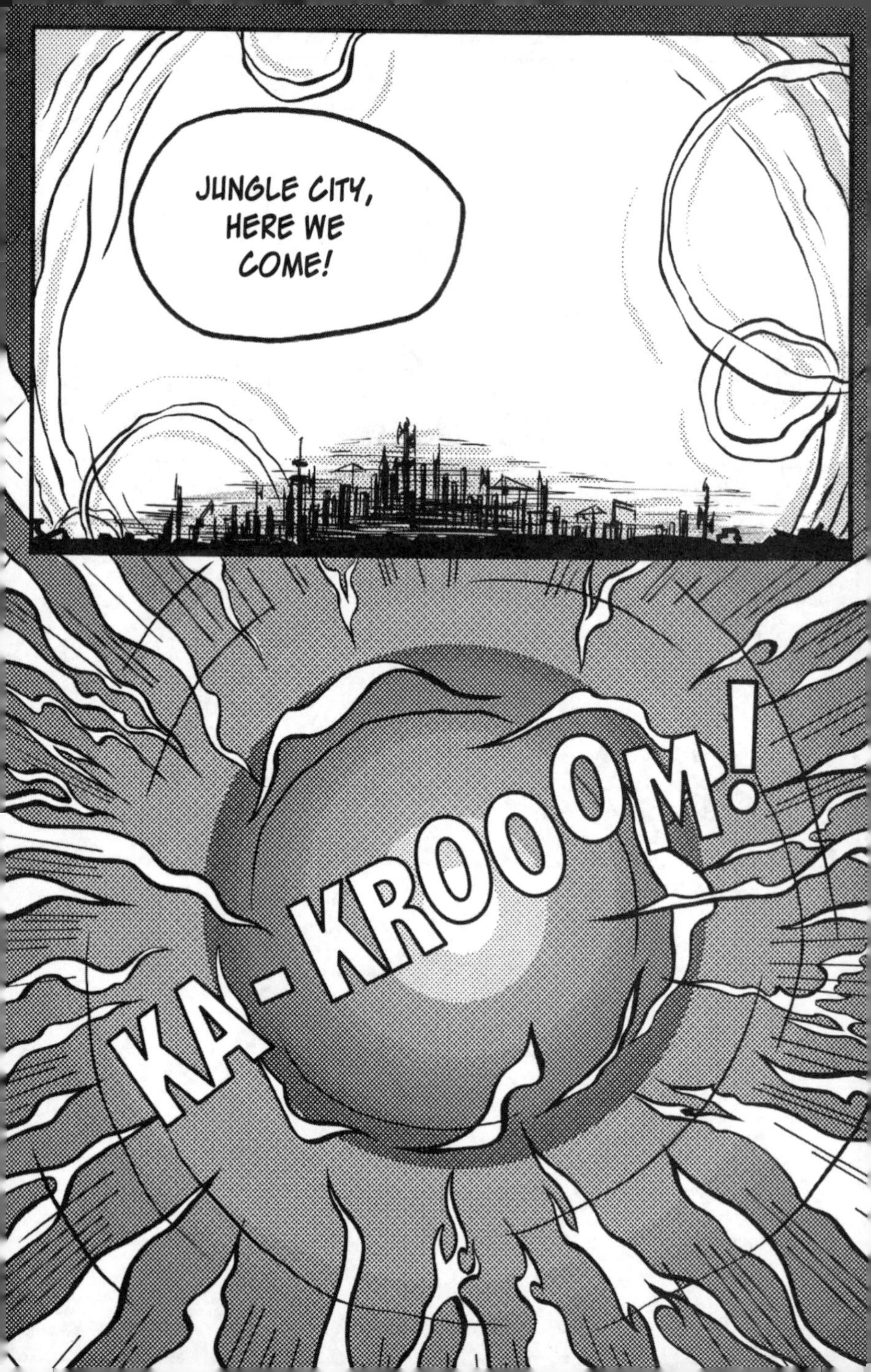
JUNGLE CITY, HERE WE COME!
KA-KROOOOM!

Chapter 9:
Endings and Beginnings

Iron City found a home in Jungle City. It fit perfectly inside the empty volcano. As word spread of how Boo, Asano, Kira, and their animal companions had saved Iron City, all the Agents came to see.

In the fresh air, the Commissars didn't need masks. Hundreds of Jungle City girls came to see them, much to their delight

"Boys!" said the Top Girl. "Jungle City has BOYS again!"

"HOOORAY!" cheered the girls.

The Commissars smiled.

"Let's punish them!" yelled one Jungle City girl.

"YEAH!" cheered all the rest.

"Oh, brother," said one of the Commissars. And they ran from the twigs and nuts that the Jungle City girls threw.

Queen Misery and Commissar Noir said very little. They were too shocked by how nice everyone was being. Everyone welcomed them, even the Supreme Agent.

"You mean, you don't hate me?" Misery asked.

"No," said the Supreme Agent. "I hated some of the things you did—but never you."

"Oh," said Misery, a smile on her face.

"Um, Miss Misery," said Agent Boo, "would you like some cake? The Top Girl made it."

"Ooh, chocolate!" said Misery. "Thank you, Agent Boo! Thank you for everything!"

Pumpkin looked over at the smiling Queen. "You know, we can't call her 'Misery' anymore."

"Well, my real name's Melanie," Misery said.

"What a pretty name!" said the Supreme Agent. "Everyone, may I present Queen *Melanie* of Iron City!"

"To Queen Melanie!" cheered everyone.

"And to Agent Boo and her friends!" cheered the happy Melanie.

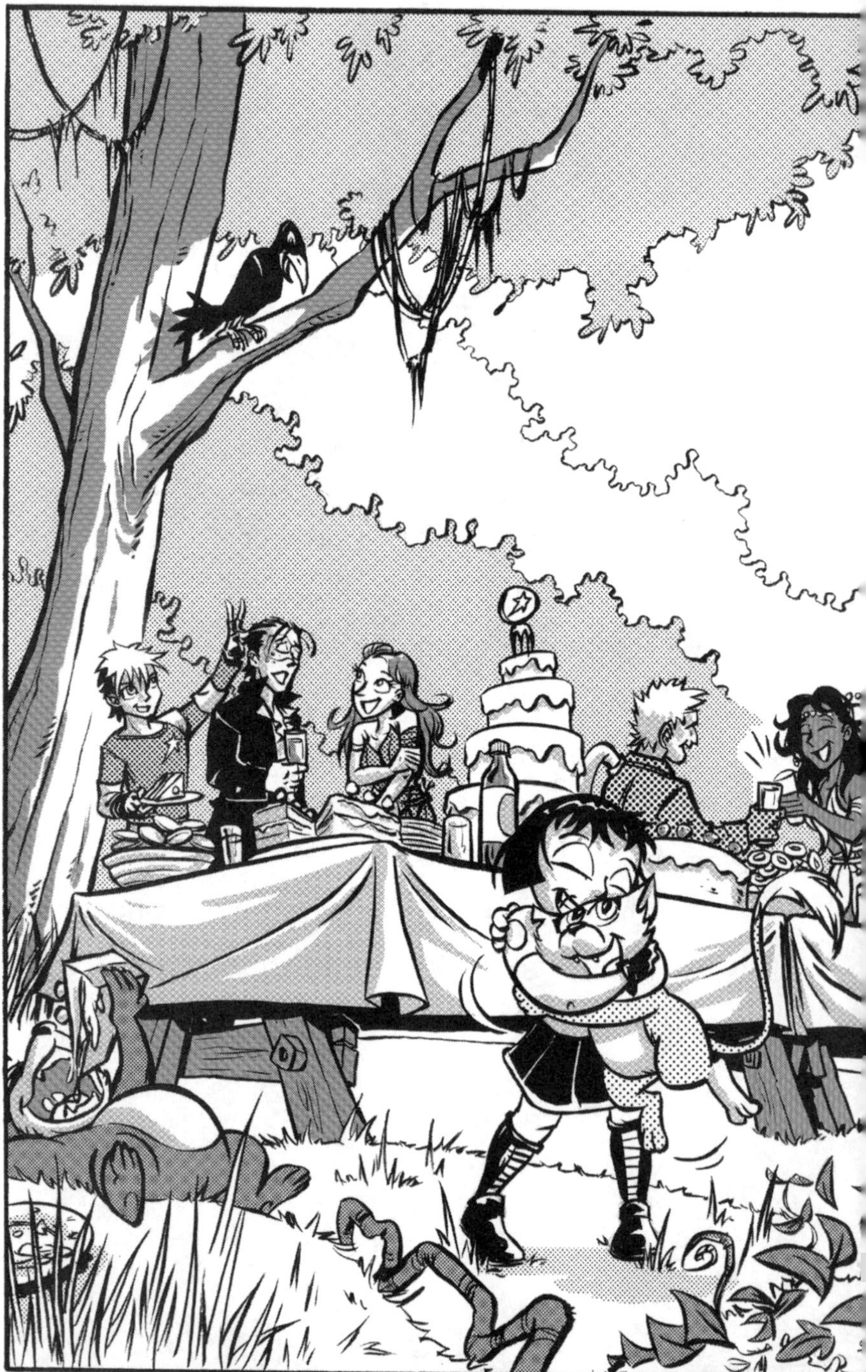

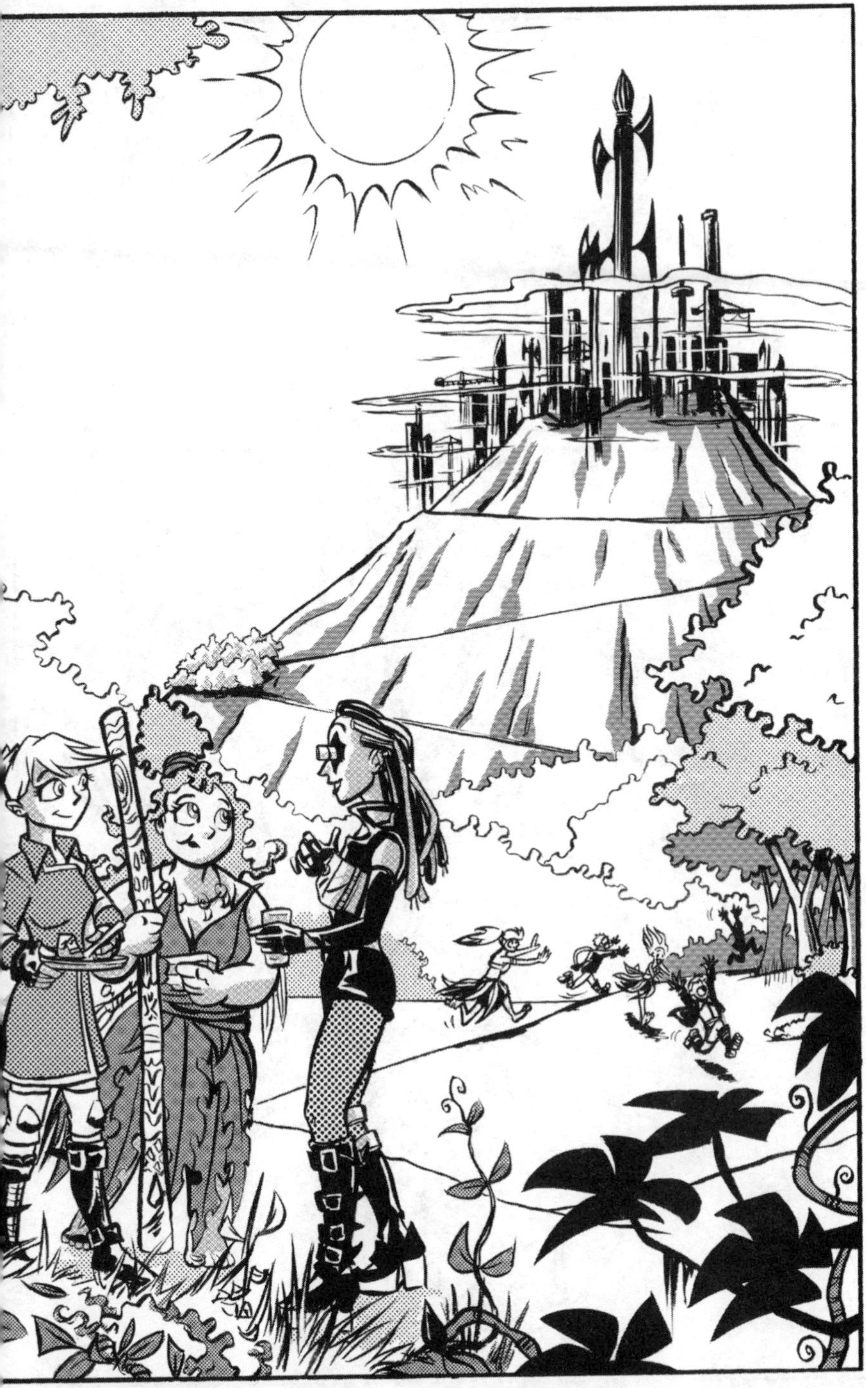

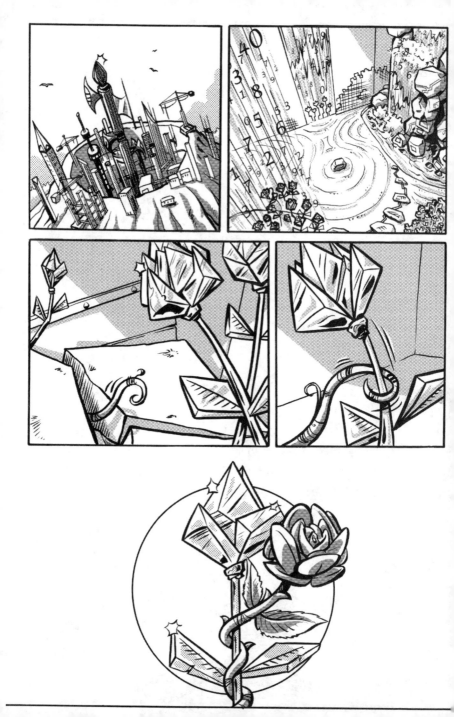